Invocations

Barbara Winkes

For D.

Chapter One

The small amusement park, abandoned almost a decade ago, was only days away from being completely demolished. A new building would go up the next year, the property making room for a skyscraper and a parking lot.

It was the last opportunity for Randy and Todd to hide between the remains of the funhouse and the merry-go-round carousel and get high. It wasn't much of a dare since they never encountered anyone. In fact, the surroundings were fairly relaxing, though one time Todd had been sure one of the horses was coming off the carousel, galloping straight towards him. Nowadays, they had a better supply, better quality, and this kind of thing didn't happen anymore. They hung out, had a few beers and talked.

Outside the fence, excavators and other heavy machinery were already parked, signs of irreversible change to come. Todd found the usual entry through the broken part of the fence. Not even a stray cat came here anymore.

It was truly the end of an era, he thought. Perhaps he should change some things in his life as well.

Randy was already there, and they settled into their usual spot, a rackety picnic table where once a food truck stood. The night was unusually mild. He had read about climate change. If the world was about to go to hell in a handbasket, they might as

1

well go out on a high. He didn't mean that literally, of course. Todd had plans.

"Hey, you're late," Randy said, handing him a beer. "Girlfriend keeping you?"

"No. She's working tonight."

He and Lisa were saving up to get out of their tiny apartment into a better place. Needless to say, she didn't know how much money he'd spent on tonight's entertainment. But this, him and Randy at the park, was a tradition. You didn't let go of something like that lightly.

He sat down and drank, enjoying the bitter taste of the beer.

"This will all be gone soon," he said. "It's a shame."

Randy laughed. "You're all sentimental tonight? This place was convenient, but neither of us ever saw it in action."

"Not the point." He clinked his bottle against Randy's. "To traditions."

"Whatever. Cheers."

Randy was right, he was too young to remember when the place had still been in business, but looking at that old sad carousel, he could easily imagine. He and Lisa might have kids someday. Some things they took for granted might be gone forever.

The sound startled him out of his thoughts, but when he looked over to Randy, he found his friend unconcerned. It was probably nothing. An animal that had found its way though the fence. Squirrels were chasing one another in the tree a few feet way. There it was again, and this time, he could tell from Randy's expression that he'd heard it too.

"We got company?"

"Some lost animal," Randy reasoned. He got to his feet.

"An animal with heavy footsteps. We better pack up here."

"Come on. You just don't want Lisa to find out what you're doing."

"That has nothing to do with...Do you hear that?"

The music sounded strange and out of place, more suitable for a circus performance about to start. A chill ran down his spine. This was ridiculous. With Halloween only a few weeks away, someone was trying to play a prank on them.

"Hey, whatever you're trying to do, it's not working!" Randy called. "Losers!"

"Let's leave," Todd suggested. He had a bad feeling. "We can go to my place. Lisa won't be home before midnight."

"All right." With an exaggerated sigh, Randy picked up the six pack.

Todd made sure they didn't leave any of their other means of entertainment behind. Despite his promise, he might try to get rid of it. Lisa wouldn't be happy to find drugs of any kind at their place. He and Randy mostly stuck to pot, but the last day at the park was supposed to be special.

The last day.

"Let's go!"

They headed back the way they had come in, past the rusty turnstile and towards the fence. That was where they saw them.

A group of four—men, he assumed, though he couldn't tell for sure. The newcomers were dressed in costumes, *clown* costumes, and full make-up. They were carrying duffle bags.

Todd froze, instantly understanding that this wasn't just a harmless prank. Harm coming to them was getting more likely by the second.

"Run," he shouted, turned around and did his best to put distance between him and the creepy group. Behind him, he heard frantic footsteps which, Todd assumed, belonged to Randy. He couldn't bring himself to look back. This was infinitely worse than his hallucination starring the carousel horse. Those clowns were real. Or were they?

Eventually, the sound of the music and the footsteps became fainter. Before Todd headed for cover in the remaining walls of the funhouse, he saw Randy running in the other direction. They always used the same entrance, because there was a wall on the other end, but perhaps they could get over it? Todd looked around for anything he could use as a weapon. How likely was it that they could placate the clowns with some beer and the coke he'd scored for tonight?

Todd turned around, nearly going out of his skin when he saw the reflection of the clown in the broken mirror. That was just a fainted illustration on the wall behind him. Not the real thing. The night was quiet again, making him wonder if he had imagined this whole episode. Had he started on the fun by himself, before Randy arrived? Made up their conversation about traditions and such...?

Todd jumped, slapping his hand against his mouth when the shot rang out, and a scream followed. He cowered next to the broken mirror, his mind frantic.

Why tonight? Why us? Please don't kill me, was his last thought before the world went black.

❦

A fussy and hungry baby had made for an early start in the Carpenter/Harding household, but now Meri was back asleep. Sunday morning at six a.m., the house was quiet, the two of them back in their own bed. It was the first time in a while that they'd be able to sleep in, with no immediate plans. Ellie sighed in bliss when Jordan's lips touched her neck, warm hands stealing under her nightgown.

"I thought we might catch up on some sleep, but I think this could go either way," she whispered.

Jordan laughed softly. "If we're efficient enough, we can do both." Her explorations had already gone far beyond cuddling.

Ellie's breath caught as she smiled in the dark.

"There's no question."

Between tender kisses that soon turned passionate, they undressed each other. Ellie reveled in the pure pleasure of the intimate moment. She'd fallen hard for Jordan Carpenter the day they met, and from that day, there had been no looking back and no regrets. She was only more in love, and incredibly proud of what they had achieved together, a home, and a family.

Contrary to the occasional warnings, their busy lives had not kept them from amazing sex. Like now. She tried to focus on the feel of Jordan's warm skin against her own, fingertips teasing and tantalizing...

Sunday morning at six, there was no reason why her boss would pop into her mind, or Jill Allen, a reporter who had first warned her of dire things to come. Redistricting, budget cuts, possible downsizing. Ellie had been the last detective to be hired into her unit. The headlines had died down, but the talk among colleagues hadn't.

"Are you still with me?" Jordan sounded reasonably concerned, and a tad amused.

"Of course! Sorry. I got a bit distracted. I'm sorry."

Jordan ran a gentle hand down her back. "You're not going to get fired. That talk comes up every once in a while. Just ignore it."

"But what if? We could pay the mortgage, but it would be a lot tighter."

"There's no point in going there. Worst case scenario, you'd be transferred. I don't think that's going to happen."

"When did you become the optimistic one?" Ellie wondered out loud. That hadn't come out right. Fortunately, Jordan wasn't offended.

"When I see no reason to worry, and that should tell you something. Now, is there anything else we need to discuss, or would you like me to—" Jordan didn't finish the sentence as Ellie pulled her down to her. "I guess the answer is yes."

"It is."

This time, when she closed her eyes, no images of Lieutenant Carroll or Jill came up. All her attention centered on Jordan's renewed and successful efforts to distract Ellie from her worries. She bit her lip, surrendering to the irresistible touch of lips and fingertips, her own fingers tangling in Jordan's hair.

The only thing she was going to see were stars.

Everything was going to be all right.

Chapter Two

R oll call Monday morning started with a surprise, though not the bad one that Ellie had feared. It wasn't a good one either. Jordan stood next to their friends and colleagues, Detectives Henderson and Doss, as Sergeant Bristol filled in the officers.

"In the past couple of weeks, we've had a few smaller incidents in the vicinity. It seems that they've moved to the city. So far, we have concerned parents and a couple of near accidents related to clown sightings."

Maria Doss, who had taken a sip of her coffee, nearly choked, and several of the officers in the room snickered. Jordan wasn't sure if the situation called for amusement. Bristol's delivery was a tad too sober for that. He wouldn't bring up this subject three weeks before Halloween if it wasn't serious. Those occurrences might be meant as a prank, but someone could get easily hurt. She suppressed a sigh. They didn't need this on top of the normal workload, but like full moon nights, holidays didn't always bring out the best in people. As Bristol continued relating details, and what to watch out for, she noticed Derek shudder.

"Come on, you're not afraid of clowns?" she whispered in disbelief. "I thought we'd seen it all." It felt like that some days, though this was new, at least for their department.

"I'm not scared," he returned with righteous indignation. "They are creepy."

"Like I said." Bristol gave his audience a stern look, "This is not a joke. Halloween is around the corner, and while most people are interested in harmless fun, some get inspired. Be aware."

They walked out behind a group of officers, in time to hear Chris Atwood say to his partner, "They bring in detectives for this? Must be really slow upstairs." The other officer shrugged. Atwood went on. "I wonder if this has to do with the coming budget cuts. It's a bit silly. We have a real job to do out there. We're not the ones wasting money."

"That's enough," Bristol chided him. "Atwood, you do have a job. Go do it."

"You really think this could become a problem? Clowns?" Jordan asked the sergeant when Atwood and his partner were out of earshot.

"You tell me, Detective. So far, we have a few scared children and a young man treated for shock after he nearly crashed his car. A woman in a parking garage." He hesitated only for a second. "If it stops here, that's fine by me."

"Me too. We're going to take our daughter trick-or-treating for the first time."

"Enjoy the moment," he said. "That time just flies by."

"It does," Jordan agreed.

They headed back to their desks where Jordan noticed that Lieutenant Carroll's office was still dark. In recent weeks, he had done everything he could to ward off the never-ending rumors. If the media picked up the story of clowns haunting the city, that might help.

She started to work on a report, then cast a curious glance at Derek who had done the same.

"We probably won't even see one of those, but is there a story I should be aware of?"

He knew exactly what she was talking about. "Leave it alone. As long as they aren't killing anyone, or trying to, it's none of our business. It's not my favorite holiday either."

"Well, look on the bright side. A couple of weeks, and it will be over."

"Yeah. Fortunately."

Leaning back in her seat, Jordan remembered that there had been little to no trick-or-treating early in her life, and by the time the Carpenters had taken her in, it was almost too late. She wanted to make every holiday special for Meri, even if it was early. She went back to the report, finished another one and made a few calls before she got up to get herself a coffee.

The break room was unusually crowded. Atwood stood in a corner with a couple of other officers.

Ellie had come in later today after getting Meri ready to spend the day at her grandparents'. She was standing by the sitting area with Maria who jumped when out of nowhere, the rubber spider appeared on the table right in front of Ellie.

Atwood was cracking up with laughter, the other two with him quickly curbing their amusement when Sergeant Bristol thundered, "What is this, a kindergarten? Atwood, why are you even here?"

Atwood's face reddened as he answered, "Sir. I'm sorry. This was just—"

"Leave it and get back to work. All of you." He shook his head. "Sorry, Harding." Bristol left without getting anything.

"Wow," Maria said. "I know he's a child, but in my house, someone else always takes care of these things. It's the reason I got a cat. Could one of you put this away please?"

"A cat? That's new." Ellie tossed the offending object in the trash can. "Better?"

"Yeah, I got him last month. Thank you. This is not how I wanted to start the day."

They would all have better days once Atwood moved on, Jordan thought. Unfortunately, he had shown no signs of wanting to do so.

A knock on the doorframe preceded Derek into the room. "Carroll is here now. He wants to see all of us," he said, sounding serious.

Jordan and Ellie exchanged a quick glance. Ellie looked as startled as Maria had a moment ago. It occurred to Jordan that they might be confronted with something scarier than clowns or silly pranks.

They would be able to keep the house, either way. She touched Ellie's shoulder, hoping to convey confidence and comfort, not sure whether she had succeeded.

"Can't get much worse," Maria commented.

Todd couldn't see anything. He had no means of reference, nothing to tell him where he was and with whom. At first, he thought he might be blindfolded, or worse, blind, but after a few moments, he could make out shapes, tensing immediately.

He was cold and hungry, lying on a hard uneven surface digging into his shoulder. Pain. He had learned something. The shapes meant pain.

Lieutenant Carroll stood in front of his office. To Jordan's surprise, Lieutenant Daniels of Major Crimes was also present.

There was a chance this had nothing to do with the persisting rumors. They had arrested Noah Shriver, a former detective who had murdered two people and spent months on the run, not long ago. He had worked in Daniels' Major Crimes unit.

Did she have any news? Jordan hoped this case didn't mean any repercussions for the department. They had used every possible resource to bring him in. She perched on the edge of her desk, aware of Ellie tense and quiet next to her.

"Everyone's here now, good. Let's start."

Lt. Daniels gave a tense smile. Carroll continued.

"As you all know, there have been many rumors about the future of the department floating around. Lieutenant Daniels and I want to put an end to all of this now."

Jordan wasn't sure if that was enough reason to be relieved. The atmosphere in the room felt different to her.

"First of all, I want you to inform that I'm going to retire at the end of this month." He held up his hand when the background noise level rose all of a sudden. No one had expected this. What the hell did it mean? The whispered words she could make out echoed Jordan's thoughts exactly.

There had been attempts to place the blame, for the Waters affair, for cases the public thought weren't solved quickly enough. But Waters had been dealt with. If Carroll had been slow to react, they all shared that blame. Too long they had thought of him as a nuisance rather than an imminent danger. This couldn't be the reason?

"Quiet, please. This decision was made after much deliberation. It's an honor to have worked with all of you. If you must know, I also look forward to spending more time with my grandchildren."

That elicited some laughter from the group assembled, though the tension wasn't entirely gone.

"Lieutenant Daniels will take over the first of next month, but she'll spend the coming weeks here with us to get caught up."

"You're leaving Major Crimes?" Maria asked.

Many other questions hung in the air, regarding Shriver and whatever his case might have to do with these sudden changes.

"A couple of my detectives will come with me, others will transfer to Vice and Narcotics," Daniels confirmed. "It's been decided that this will be the most efficient way for us to work."

Her use of passive voice indicated to everyone in the room that not all of those changes had been her choice, or those of her unit. They had yet to determine if increased efficiency would be the result. Nevertheless, Homicide meant a step up for Daniels. It wasn't entirely clear what it meant for the rest of them.

Finally, Derek asked. "Do we have to expect any...downsizing here as well?"

"No." Carroll's answer was swift. "In fact, we'll have to cover a slightly larger area which means we need everyone."

"I see. Thank you, sir." When Carroll turned to Daniels, Derek whispered to Jordan, "Which means, they should be hiring but won't, and this is the best they could do. I wonder if they'll make us share a desk. It's crowded as it is."

"Yeah."

Ellie looked relieved, though pensive. Jordan held her gaze long enough to share a quick smile. This might not be the end of the story, but it was far from the worst-case scenario. She'd miss Carroll. She also understood that this could be an opportunity for Daniels. Based on the few encounters she'd had with the new lieutenant, Jordan had to admit she was a good choice.

However, Derek had a point as well. The space wasn't un-limited, and she assumed that the hope for increased efficiency would also mean changes in their day-to-day work, sanctioned by politicians who had to show something to their constituents, but didn't always understand the details involved. As long as they got a couple of new colleagues out of it, it wouldn't be so bad. After Waters, and Shriver, their main imperative was to get the work done and regain the public's trust.

"That's all you have to say?"

"Shh," she made in his direction when Daniels spoke again.

"Now that we've covered this, I just wanted to let you know that I want to talk to each one of you, for the best possible transition. I'd like to start tomorrow morning with Detectives Henderson and Carpenter."

"In order of job security?" Ellie mumbled, only for Jordan to overhear.

"Stop it," Jordan whispered back. Louder, she said. "Of course. We'll make the time." She and Derek had a reputation when it came to closed cases. Daniels had wished her well when she was pregnant with Meri. Jordan was willing to give her the benefit of the doubt and assume no one's job was in danger. In the past years, work hadn't been slow. Ellie had no reason to be worried, but if she still was, Jordan had her methods to distract her.

She suppressed a smile at the memory.

Daniels was interrupted by Officer Libby Marshall rushing in.

"We need someone at the hospital. A man who was just brought in reported a murder."

"Carpenter, Henderson, you go," Carroll decided. "If you have any questions later, come find me in my office."

Keys in hand, Jordan was already in her coat before he had finished talking.

"Yes, sir," Derek said, and they left.

Chapter Three

"**I** didn't know this," he said when they were in the car. "He's young to retire. You think there's something else?"

"I don't think so, but either way, we'll have to go with what they tell us. Daniels is okay. And, bright side, it's not a clown sighting."

"That's very funny."

"I'm not trying to be funny," Jordan clarified. "Look, I don't think Carroll has lied to us. Ever. He told Ellie she wouldn't lose her job. I think it's exactly what he said—he wants more family time, and I can't say I blame him. This isn't a bad thing for any of us."

"This is not what I said. I'm just cautious. And you've been unusually cheerful."

Maybe that's because for some time now, no one has tried to sue or kill me? But that would be too obvious a point to make.

"Life is good," she said vaguely. "I appreciate it."

"That is a good thing. All right, let's see what this alleged murder is all about."

They had arrived at the hospital. Jordan found a parking spot, and they exited the car and headed to the front desk.

"I'm Detective Carpenter, this is Detective Henderson," she said, showing her badge to the nurse. "We're here about Todd Williams."

15

"Dr. Romano wants to talk to you first. Give me a second?" A plastic pumpkin the size of an apple sat on the counter. Other, less understated Halloween decorations were probably inappropriate for the setting.

A few minutes later, the nurse returned with the doctor and introduced them.

"You're here, good," Romano said. "When Mr. Williams told us about the murder, we called you."

"Do you have reasons to doubt his story?" Jordan asked.

"I don't doubt that he's traumatized. He was brought in with hypothermia, and also cuts and bruises. We are running a tox screen, but I'm almost certain drugs were involved."

Jordan hadn't missed the phrasing. "Drugs that he took, or someone forced him to take?"

"You'll have to ask him. I just wanted to warn you that some things don't add up."

"What about next of kin?"

"He had no papers on him, but he gave us the number of his girlfriend, Lisa Garner. She's on her way."

"Okay. Thanks, Dr. Romano."

When they stepped into the room, Williams' eyes darted nervously from Jordan to Derek, and he only slightly calmed down when they identified themselves. He looked to be in his mid-to-late twenties, bruises and cuts marring his face and neck.

"Mr. Williams, can you tell us what happened to you?" Derek asked.

Had he gotten into a fight and lost consciousness? Had he been held somewhere?

"Is Lisa here yet? She's going to be so mad."

"She's on her way," Jordan said. "You told Dr. Romano that there has been a murder. You saw it happen?"

"I didn't say I saw it happen, but I know they shot him. Randy. We were just hanging out, having a few beers, and all of a sudden, we heard that creepy music. They were chasing us...they shot him."

"Who is they?" she asked softly.

"Clowns," he said. Jordan caught Derek's gaze as she tried to keep her expression neutral. She could feel her jaw dropping. "The creepy clowns murdered him," Williams reiterated.

"Okay, Todd, from the beginning, please. Where did this happen?" Jordan asked.

"I was afraid you wouldn't believe me," he confessed.

"We believe you all right, don't worry," Derek told him. "Like my colleague said, we need to know everything. From the start."

"All right. We met by the old amusement park. You know the one? They're going to flatten it to build an office tower."

"Hasn't the site been closed off for years?" Jordan asked.

Todd looked embarrassed. While she had an idea as to the reason why, she was also impatient. Something had obviously happened to him, and perhaps, his friend Randy. Time was ticking.

"Right now, we need to know what happened," she continued. "That's it. Like you said, they're going to tear it down. Whatever you did there, it's not important right now."

To her relief, that seemed to be enough reassurance.

"We usually got in through a hole in the fence, wandered around a bit, hung out...We got some booze and pot and...this time, I got us some coke."

Jordan suppressed a sigh. While this wasn't priority at the moment, his memory was likely to be impacted.

"Go on. Please."

"We were talking, and then we heard the sounds, like someone was coming. At first, we thought they might be squirrels but then…" He shuddered. "There was the music. We were about to head out when we saw them. Four. I remember I was yelling at Randy to run, and I think we both did. There was a gunshot, but it gets fuzzy from there. I remember…pain. Please, find who did this to him?"

"What's Randy's last name?"

"Fowler," he said. "He lives with his Grandma, Elise." They finished up the interview, and Jordan laid her card on the side table.

"Thank you, Todd. If you remember anything else, please don't hesitate to call."

"You're not going to charge me for trespassing?"

Jordan wasn't going to make any promises. If trespassing was the worst that happened, they'd all be lucky.

"Not at this point," she said. "You concentrate on getting better."

Outside the room, she told Derek, "I'd like to talk to the girlfriend, but I think that can wait until tomorrow. I want to check on Randy first."

He had no objection.

They walked along the hallway in silence until Derek spoke.

"Okay, I'm going to say it. What are the chances that they got high, ran into some trouble, got into a fight, and he imagined those clowns?"

"I keep hearing that word, and I don't like it. I'd go with your theory if we hadn't had a briefing where we were told to look out for that kind of thing. Something happened to him, and either way it's not good. This wasn't a harmless prank."

"No, it sure wasn't. Your thoughts on Randy?"

"I'd like it if he was just hiding out at his grandma's." Jordan shrugged. "We'll see. If we're really lucky, he's there and can tell us what happened." She was afraid it wasn't likely. A gunshot, that was specific. But why? Why now, if no one had bothered the two men in months?

Randy and Elise Fowler lived in an apartment building about ten minutes from the hospital. A few seconds after Jordan rang the doorbell, a woman in her early seventies opened the door to them. Halfway through their introduction, tears formed in Elise Fowler's eyes.

"Something happened to Randy, am I right?"

"What makes you think that?"

"He hasn't been home in five days," she said. "I called the police, and an officer came by, but I'm not sure they took me seriously."

Jordan barely refrained from shaking her head. This wasn't a good impression to make on any day, even less so when the department was under a lot of scrutiny.

"Do you remember the officer's name?"

"Yes," Mrs. Fowler said. "I wrote it down. Officer Atwood. Did Randy get hurt?"

This was worse. The press and the higher-ups were taking a close look as they were entitled to—and Atwood acted like he didn't care, like his screw-ups didn't reflect back on the city's force. For someone who claimed to work hard, he wasn't getting a lot done.

"We don't know yet," she admitted. "But I'm very sorry you didn't feel taken seriously. Can you tell us when you last spoke to Randy?"

With a resigned expression, Elise Fowler stepped back to let them in.

"You promise you're going to look for him?"

"That's our job, Ma'am," Derek assured her, and they went into the modestly furnished living room. "Your grandson lives with you full-time?"

"Yes," she said. "It's close to his work. He's saving on rent, and he does errands for me. He's a good man. As to your question," she directed at Jordan, "he went out with a friend. Todd. They usually go out for drinks a few times a month."

"You know Todd?"

"He works hard, like Randy. He and his girlfriend want to get out of their tiny apartment, start a family." There was renewed alarm in her expression. "He didn't get back to me, and I didn't know how to reach him. Did something happen to him?"

"We are still looking into that," Jordan said quickly. As long as they weren't sure as to Todd Williams' experiences, she didn't think it was a good idea to tell Mrs. Fowler. He didn't remember. Jordan didn't want her to jump to conclusions. "To your knowledge, did that happen before, that either one of them disappeared for a few days?"

"Of course not," the woman all but snapped at her. "Randy wouldn't do that to me."

"Do you know friends of his other than Todd?"

"I can give you the address of his work, but he mostly met with Todd."

At this point, Jordan couldn't see how they might come up with a harmless explanation for the events of the past five days. Aside from Lisa, they'd have to talk to Todd again. There was something they needed to do first.

"Yes, please. Thank you, Mrs. Fowler. We'll get back to you as soon as we learn anything."

Derek drove on the way while Jordan made some calls and pulled up a map on her phone. The site of the old amusement park. The clown sightings on the outskirts of town. The same people, or had someone jumped on the bandwagon?

"Copycat clowns?" she said out loud. "This is getting weird."

"It's getting weird? I think we're already there," Derek commented. "I don't mean to blame the victim, but I have a question. Why get high in a place that's already this creepy?"

"Beats me. All we know is that it's gotten a lot creepier. If we're lucky, this is still something to hand over to Missing Persons by the end of the day."

Chapter Four

The sky had clouded over by the time they arrived at the venue. A couple of squad cars were already parked near what used to be the entrance.

Officers Casey Lyons and Sam Potts greeted them.

"We found the place where they got through the fence," Casey said. "We were just waiting for you."

"All right. Let's do this."

As they walked along the fence surrounding broken and abandoned rides, Casey spoke, "So, what's scarier, politicians drawing lines on a map any way it suits them, or scary clowns?"

"I want to say, what's the difference, but I think that was a rhetorical question," Jordan said dryly.

"Correct on both."

They had arrived at the hole in the fence, about four feet tall and three feet wide, mostly covered in shrubs. Broken branches indicated that someone had taken this route before and done little to cover their tracks.

So far, they hadn't found anything to contradict the theory that Todd and Randy had been targeted. Like the children being scared, the woman in the parking garage, the man who almost had an accident, it seemed like a random occurrence, except for the escalation of violence. It had rained in the past couple of days. Any footprints would be lost.

They came to the place Todd had described, the picnic table, to the left, the merry-go-round, and the funhouse to the right—or what was left of them. A closer look at the table didn't show anything out of the ordinary. This was where they'd sat, drunk, smoked...and then what? Clown music. Jordan imagined them hurrying to get out of the place, then turning around when the group of four met them. Men, women? It wasn't clear yet.

She stepped inside the remaining walls of the funhouse where critters of various kinds had made a home. Weeds had taken over the space. A broken mirror reflected her scowl, distorting her features. She almost jumped at the apparition behind her, only to realize *that* clown was just a painting. It wouldn't be hard to become paranoid in a place like this, especially when drunk and high, but it was impossible to deny the facts: Todd hadn't beaten himself up. Randy Fowler was missing since the night the two of them had been here.

Confronted by clowns. She rubbed her forehead, wondering if they should take Meri out of town for a getaway rather than trick-or-treating.

Even though part of the building's roof was gone, she could still hear her colleague's voices outside, slightly muted. This was where Todd had been hiding. Not a great place, considering that there was only one entrance. Perhaps he had hoped the clowns would leave?

She crouched down and noticed dark stains on some of the shards of the mirror. Jordan didn't doubt it was blood. Looking up, she saw the reflection of movement behind her, and she was on her feet in an instant. No sound. Nothing there.

"Jordan!" she heard Derek call. She went to leave through the same door she'd come in, realizing it didn't budge.

"Where are you?"

"In here!"

The doorknob didn't move, and she changed tactics, using her whole weight against it. To no avail. It was like someone had locked it from the outside. Had someone been waiting for them—and what did they want them to find?

⁂

Eventually, the door opened, revealing Derek and Sam, their expressions grim.

"Okay, that was unplanned. It probably jammed? Did you see anyone?"

"No," he said. "But we found something."

"I did too. There's blood on this mirror, I think it's likely Todd's. They beat him up in here and then brought him elsewhere."

"Yeah. Looks like he was the lucky one."

She didn't have to ask what that meant. Jordan cringed at the sight of the tableau laid out for them behind a small stand where a sign still advertised candy cotton.

Trick or Treat was scrawled in bright orange letters on the wall. On the ground...A human hand was arranged in a way to look like it was reaching from below the earth.

"This is fucked up," she said the first thing that sprang to mind. No one disagreed with her.

"Given that Todd wasn't missing a limb, what are the odds that this is Randy Fowler's?" Derek said.

"Any other body parts?"

"Not yet, but I wouldn't be surprised."

"There's something else," Sam said. "I heard that they were going to tear down everything to start on the parking lot this week."

"Yeah, that's not going to happen now." Jordan shook her head. "Daniels picked a fun time to join us."

Ellie had spent most of the day wrapping up paperwork and a couple of interviews and keeping her head down. Jordan and Derek were handling what was now a crime scene. Daniels had begun shadowing Carroll, and the two had been gone for some time, but were back in his office.

So far, the developments hadn't been as bad as she feared. Perhaps she had overreacted. Given the fact that she was the last detective to be hired in Homicide, she still felt vulnerable with every upheaval.

She wondered how Daniels felt about Ellie being the one who had brought Shriver's case to their attention. Ellie went back to filling out the last items, startled when Daniels appeared in front of her desk.

"Lieutenant. What can I do for you?" She had a hard time not to cringe, aware of her voice sounding both eager and apprehensive.

"We're still waiting on Carpenter and Henderson, and Lieutenant Carroll had work to do that doesn't include me...I'm getting a coffee, and I was wondering if you'd like to join me."

"Sure. I could use one too." That was only marginally better.

"I know I said we'd start tomorrow, but we're here now. If you don't have anything pressing at the moment, we could talk."

Jordan would tell her she was paranoid, but for a split-second, Ellie's imagination got the better of her. "Now's a good time." It was all she could do not to blurt out something entirely different.

"Great. Please remember this is not an interview or anything. I got myself up to date, but to be able to do the job the best I can, I want to familiarize myself more with each of you, and the way you work."

"I understand that." Ellie held back the comment that she, too, had to find a way to fit herself into the tightly knit unit. Daniels probably wasn't as worried about fitting in. She was going to be their boss.

They went to get a coffee from the break room, and Daniels took her to an office across the hall, where they sat down. Ellie waited.

"I studied up on your latest cases, who worked with whom, et cetera. You were partnered with Detective Waters at first."

"Yes. You know what happened...I believe everyone knows."

"Of course. And then, after that?"

"I helped out wherever I was needed. I often worked with Detective Doss, even though we're not officially partners."

"Right." Daniels looked thoughtful, making Ellie wonder if she'd said something wrong. "I think it would be a good idea if we made it official."

"Sure, that would be great. Is there anything...I should be worried about?"

"No, not at all. Your work is beyond reproach. I noticed that sometimes it was just your signature on a report, and it wasn't clear whether you worked with a senior detective."

Ellie suppressed a sigh. None of her colleagues enjoyed paperwork, but she knew that Waters had been downright sloppy at times.

"A few times, you worked alongside your wife...It could be seen as problematic. We should be able to improve here, especially with two new detectives. I understand the necessity sometimes, but it would be better if we could avoid that in the future."

"I see what you mean." Again, those assignments had been made beyond her control, when time was of the essence. "And I know you're right."

Daniels had sensed her hesitation.

"Please don't get me wrong. Waters wasn't your fault."

"Shriver wasn't yours either," Ellie said, aware a split-second later that she'd overstepped. Lieutenant Daniels handled her comment gracefully.

"I think we're all glad this part of the system still works, even if it took a while. I'll talk to Detective Doss."

"Thank you, Lieutenant."

"You're welcome. That will be all for now."

Things weren't going be worse, but they sure wouldn't stay the same, Ellie reflected as she walked back to her desk. That, she could live with. Beyond reproach. Ellie smiled to herself. She hadn't known how much she needed to hear these words until Daniels had said them out loud.

Jordan was more than grateful that neither of them had to take care of dinner when they could finally make it home. Kate McCarthy, their friend and Derek Henderson's wife, had been babysitting Meri.

Jordan and Ellie got to tuck in their daughter and say goodnight. When she was asleep, they joined Kate and Derek downstairs to order dinner.

After the hours spent on the uneven terrain and filling in the CSU crew they had notified after the gruesome find, Jordan appreciated the downtime.

"So, how was your day?" Kate asked. "I keep hearing something about people seeing clowns. That's a hoax, right?"

"I wish," Jordan answered, while Derek added, "We don't have to talk about this over dinner, right?"

"I'm good with that. Beer, everyone?" she asked.

She got appreciative nods all around, except from Kate. "These exams are kicking my ass. I'll get up very early tomorrow."

"Okay. I guess we will too, if Daniels wants to talk to us early. This should be interesting."

Ellie followed her into the kitchen where she said, "I had my meeting with her already. It was okay, very informal."

"Really." Jordan leaned back against the counter. "What did she say?"

"She'd like me to work with Maria in the future. Just in case someone might think I haven't gotten enough supervision...and also because I've been working with my wife on too many occasions."

"Yeah, she's right about that. We had no choice at the time, but I guess Carroll would have done the same eventually." She shook her head. "It's a challenge, no doubt, but it must be strange that she got her unit taken away."

Their conversation was interrupted by the doorbell.

"I'll get it," Jordan said. Heading to the front door, she acknowledged a sense of relief, despite the long day. She didn't think anyone could have let Ellie go in good conscience, but she might have had to transfer. It was good to know that the powers that be considered everyone necessary.

Chapter Five

The search of the premises hadn't turned up more body parts. While they were waiting for the results of the DNA testing, Derek went to see Lieutenant Daniels. Jordan called Todd's girlfriend Lisa Garner.

Lisa agreed to come in during her lunch break.

"How's Todd?" Jordan asked.

"It's hard to say," Lisa admitted. "He's scared. Did you find who did this to him?"

"We're still looking."

"I hope you'll get them soon. I've never seen him so scared." Jordan saw Derek leave the lieutenant's office, looking thoughtful.

"He's been through a traumatic experience. It's normal." She didn't want to ask Lisa any difficult questions on the phone. It wasn't only to be kind. Jordan didn't want to give her too much time to think about her answers or come up with a different version if there was one. Lisa sounded genuinely concerned, but Jordan would make up her mind when she talked to her in person.

"I guess so. I'm afraid I have to go. I'll be there at about 12:30."

"I appreciate it," Jordan said promised. "I'll see you later."

Before she could talk to Derek, Daniels was heading her way in a brisk step.

"Detective Carpenter."

"It's my turn." She kept her tone neutral, confident that there was no way anyone could argue with her and Derek's record in the time they'd worked together. A literal record. Ellie was fine, she'd be too.

Inside the office, Daniels gestured for her to sit down. This looked a little more formal, but only, Jordan assumed, because Carroll didn't need the space this morning. On occasion, they had even talked about more private subjects, when Jordan was pregnant.

"Okay, thank you for making the time. Like I told Detective Harding, and I'm sure she told you, I want to get a sense of how you've been working. You and Detective Henderson have quite the impressive record, including a number of high-profile cases."

"Thank you."

"You're welcome. The methods might have been unorthodox at times, but the results speak for themselves. And I've been where you are. Sometimes we have no choice."

At this point, Jordan was almost sure that another but was about to come. She wondered where Daniels was going with this.

"Please know that I'm not questioning your professional skills or integrity. That's not what we're here for. I'm simply trying to get the whole picture. Something that happened a couple of months ago, with a victim's parents?"

Jordan barely suppressed a groan. She should have known that these conversations would be far from idle chit-chat. It was no secret that Daniels had to answer many questions in the wake of Shriver's case. Of course she wanted to start with a slate as clean as possible.

"They asked me to apologize, and I did. There really isn't more to the story. We told a woman that her son was murdered, and she said he was dead to them already...Because he was gay. I crossed a line. It won't happen again."

In retrospect, Jordan knew she should have acted differently. The people in question needed to hear the reproach of their bigoted ways from someone, but she hadn't been in the best position to get the message across.

"I get it. And like I said, I just want to make sure I know what exactly happened here."

"It's over. They let it go after that."

"Good. That's really all I need to know."

Jordan had the unpleasant feeling that the conversation wasn't over yet. As long as she didn't go *there*...

"I'd understand if you don't want to talk about it, and I'm trying to keep it brief."

Here we go. Jordan braced herself.

"Your rescue of Judy Lawrence was quite sensationalized in the media. I read your report, and I heard a few different versions."

"She was severely injured, could barely make it out of that basement. I took a huge risk, and there were consequences. I had my talk with IA before I came back to work."

"I'm not asking you for remorse, Detective." Daniels' tone was even. "You saved that woman's life. I'm not surprised Lieutenant Carroll was able to ignore all the noise surrounding that case. I'm trying to get a complete picture. I have to know my team."

"I understand. And believe me, I wish there had been an alternative. There wasn't."

"I don't want to spend any more time on this than absolutely necessary, but it's not a secret that we'll all be under a lot of scrutiny for some time to come. I just want you to be aware of it. You could go far, in this department, or anywhere."

"Thank you. I promise you, we're all aware."

"Okay. I'm glad we understand each other."

"That's all?"

"It is. I am happy to be working with you."

Finally, the conversation was about to wind down.

"Same here, Lieutenant," Jordan said. She didn't care if it sounded a bit cheeky. Daniels' raised an eyebrow, a hint of amusement in her expression, but she didn't comment.

"Good. Thank you for your time, Detective. I'll let you get back to work."

Jordan held back a relieved sigh. "Thank you," she said as she got to her feet.

***

"Okay, this seems to be the season of mysterious murders with no real motive," Maria declared. "Neighbor called because of the smell. Who's with me?"

Ellie jumped to her feet so quickly Maria laughed.

"Are you sure?"

Reminded of her conversation with Daniels, Ellie thought it was never too early to make her see she was eager to go along with her plans.

"Yes, sure. I'll be okay."

Jordan was nowhere to be seen, and Derek was working on something at his desk when they left.

"You're that eager to get out of here?" Maria asked. "Fleeing from the new boss?"

"Oh no, she's okay. Actually, I talked to her yesterday, and she thinks we should be partners." Ellie hesitated. "I know you liked working alone..."

"I liked not having to work with Waters. You, me, that is a good idea."

"You think so?" Finally, things were falling back into place.

"Hey, no one's been let go, that's a great development. No one's going to break up Derek and Jordan, and I like this much better than a new guy telling me what to do." She laughed. "Instead, to a certain extent, I can tell *you* what to do. It will be a great new experience. Now, let's go see what I'm afraid is a partly decomposed body."

"Worse than a severed hand?"

Maria shrugged. "We'll have yet to see."

The one-story family house was part of a cozy suburban neighborhood. They passed a kindergarten and a church on the way. The only thing out of the ordinary, though telling, was the squad car parked on the curb. Ellie suppressed a sigh when she saw Atwood standing next to it, looking bored.

"If he does another stupid prank, I'm going to punch him," Maria declared as she parked behind him. Ellie didn't think she needed to say out loud that she wholeheartedly agreed.

They exited the car and greeted Atwood and his partner.

"Okay, what do we have?" Maria asked.

"Like I said already," Atwood had the audacity to start with. "Ronald Jenkins. Seems like a strange bird. He moved into the neighborhood a few years ago, but no one has seen him much. Neighbors have talked to him every once in a while, the Brenners over there," he pointed to the house next door, "brought over leftover food sometimes. I guess they took pity on him."

"Not the point. Could you please get to it?" Maria's tone was still polite, but her impatience shone through. They had all gotten impatient with his attitude.

"Woman next door has a key," he said curtly. "She went over to bring some stew, noticed the smell and went right back out to call the police. She didn't get further than the mudroom."

He held up the key, dangling it in front of them.

Holding back the impulse to roll her eyes, Ellie took it, and they hurried to Jenkins' front door. She unlocked it, and they had barely set foot inside when the smell hit them. Mrs. Brenner had been right to notify the police.

"It's a bit stuffy for sure," Maria remarked. She and Ellie had both donned gloves, and Ellie carefully turned the knob of the next door, likely to lead to some living area.

"Mr. Jenkins?" she called.

Maria's gaze was sympathetic. Ellie shrugged. She opened the door, and for a few seconds, they both stared in shock.

They couldn't see a body, or part of it, their vision obstructed by piles of magazines and other papers, stacked furniture and various knickknacks. This was something Ellie had so far only seen on TV, pausing briefly on a reality show while zapping…A thin layer of dust covered most of it.

"All right," she said, shaking herself out of her stunned state. "I guess he's in here somewhere."

"Yeah," Maria agreed. "Poor guy. What are the odds something fell on him? How does anyone live like this?"

"At some point you don't see a way out? It seems like that's what happened."

"Likely. How about we get some help in here and start clearing a path? The sooner we get him out of here, the better."

Atwood and his colleague looked a tad pale, but they, too, started to attack the towering piles.

"Be careful, don't hurt yourself." Ellie said. "We have no idea what's in there."

For once, Chris Atwood didn't scoff at her words, and she wasn't surprised. She was fairly sure that neither of them had seen anything like it. When she was still in uniform, Ellie had been called to the scene of a pile-up, where several people had been trapped in their cars. This was different. It looked like Ronald Jenkins had been trapped some time before his death.

They worked side by side, until they made it to the back of the room and got their first look at the body. Ellie carefully stepped past a partial bloody shoeprint in the carpet to open the window. She noticed the smear on the windowsill right away.

"Maria!"

"Right here," Maria said. "So that's how they got out."

"I think so," Ellie agreed. The window had given easily, which would be the case if someone had simply pushed it shut behind them. Had they left it open, someone might have noticed the smell earlier. She turned back to the victim.

Thanks to the alert neighbor, not as much time had passed as they'd feared, but the man in his early sixties was definitely dead, part of his head covered by a heavy lamp. There was blood around his head...and a lot more underneath him.

"Wow, this is different." Behind her, medical examiner Dr. Melissa Adams had arrived. "An accident?"

Ellie stepped back to let her do her work. "Unlikely," she said, pointing to the partial shoeprint. "Someone else was in here. If we're lucky, they left more behind than that print."

"The man was basically surrounded by piles of trash. Why would anyone want to kill him?" Maria mused out loud.

Dr. Adams shrugged. "I guess the question is rhetorical since it's your job to find out. Would you rather be occupied with the clowns and the severed hand?"

Maria looked thoughtful. "As long as we can get out of here and breathe some fresh air soon, I guess I'll take Mr. Jenkins here."

"I thought so."

A few hours later, the situation was marginally improved as the processing of the scene went on. Every window was open, letting in some fresher air, and Dr. Adams' team had removed the body. Boxes of evidence had been bagged and were on their way to the department.

Most of the blood likely came from a stab wound. Intimate, personal. Shuddering, Ellie pushed the thought aside as she searched the other rooms. A bedroom with a bed that looked like it hadn't been slept in for a while, clothes and other laundry piled up on it. She wondered if Mr. Jenkins could have benefited from one of those reality shows where the host tried to get to the root of the problem. Did they create long-lasting change for anyone, or questionable entertainment? Wasn't it better to deal with those issues in a safer, more private setting?

In Jenkins' case, the neighbors' efforts had only done so much. He had never let Mrs. Brenner past the mudroom.

She went through the drawers, stopping when she found the address book. Jenkins did have a landline and a laptop, and older model. She hoped that the latter would give them some insight as to who had done him harm. This was interesting.

She found the phone number of a Dr. Hoffman, and the business card of a pharmacy. Most pages were empty, though one of them said "Judy" with a local number.

"Look at this." She showed the page to Maria. "So far, the only thing personal."

"Except for this." Maria had a find of her own, a photograph showing a younger Jenkins with a woman and a child of about ten years old. "What are the odds that Judy is the woman in the picture? Maybe they got divorced."

"Let's find out."

Chapter Six

"You've been awfully quiet since you left the lieutenant's office," Derek remarked. "Anything I should prepare for?"

They were on their way to see Randy's employer, the owner of a garage close by. Lisa, Todd's girlfriend, wasn't able to add much to the story. He had left to meet with Randy. She didn't see him again until after the hospital called.

"No, not really," Jordan said, aware she was being evasive. Much of her conversation with Daniels still lingered on her mind, the subjects ranging from flattering to sobering. Carroll had backed her up, smoothed over what could have been a longer story with the ignorant parents of a serial killer's victim. And of course, Daniels was meticulous, so she had to bring up the other serial killer.

Going down to that basement on a hunch, without backup.

"I don't want to spend any more time on this than absolutely necessary, but it's not a secret that we'll all be under a lot of scrutiny for some time to come. I just want you to be aware of it. You could go far, in this department, or anywhere."

A few months ago, Jordan had been grateful to be alive, with her family, and to be able to go back to work. More than once, she had declined a job offer that her ex, Dr. Bethany Roberts, a psychiatrist with the FBI, had brought to her. Daniels had given her a lot to think about.

"That doesn't sound very convincing."

"It's true. We're fine, for now. Basically, she let me know that the higher-ups are watching her, and by proxy, us, so we better do everything by the letter of the book. No more making waves for a while."

"Right." Derek laughed, incredulous. "I get where she is coming from, so I don't blame her. I guess we have to ask the more notorious criminals to stay out of town. Just so everything goes smoothly."

"Worth a try, huh? I could do smooth for a while."

Ellie had hinted at what Daniels had told her, but they didn't have a lot of time to discuss it. Jordan wondered if she'd received the same warnings/compliments about a bright future with the department. Then again, Ellie had nothing to worry about. Whenever she had gone above the job description, it was with the backing of a supervisor.

"I wouldn't mind it," he agreed.

"Exactly. She also complimented us on our record."

"I guess that's a good thing. All right, we're here. Let's see if these folks have anything for us."

They entered the building through the reception area. The woman behind the counter got up from her chair.

"How can I help you?" she asked.

Jordan showed her badge. "Detective Carpenter, this is Detective Henderson. We're here to see Mr. Quentin."

"Just a moment, please." She never lost the pleasant smile as she turned away and went through a door in the back.

A few minutes later, she returned with a man in his fifties. He was wearing jeans and a button-down shirt.

"Detectives. You're here about Randy, I assume. Is he...?"

Jordan and Derek shared a look. Aware of the receptionist and a couple of customers waiting, she said, "Could we go somewhere more private?"

"Of course. Let's take this to my office."

Once they'd closed the door behind themselves, he asked again, "So, Homicide, that's serious. What happened to Randy?"

"We were hoping you could help us," Jordan said. "I assume people noticed he didn't show up at work?"

"Right. Sara, you just met her, she called his place. His grandmother was worried, and eventually, she filed a police report. That's all I know."

"Did he ever have problems with any of the staff? Got into arguments or fights?"

"Oh, no." Mr. Quentin shook his head, looking as if she'd suggested something outrageous. He was—is a good guy. No. I can't imagine...My staff is very dedicated, customer oriented. They don't get into arguments on the job."

"Okay. This might sound odd, but are you aware of anyone on your team being into dressing up? Specifically, as clowns?"

It was hard to ask this question with a straight face, but Jordan had a reason. She thought Quentin's reaction was a bit delayed as he laughed.

"If they do, I have no idea. Anyway, have you looked around outside? Halloween is coming."

"You're right about that. Thanks, Mr. Quentin. If you can think of anything else, please let us know."

"Wait, you didn't tell me...Randy, is he dead?"

The detail of the severed hand hadn't been released to the press yet, and they were still waiting for the test results.

"We can't say for sure yet," Derek told him. "Thank you."

On the way back, they stopped for a quick coffee at a local chain.

"What a waste of time," Derek said as they sat down with their beverages.

"Maybe not," Jordan argued. "I counted four duffel bags in the corner of the office."

"Damn. Four clowns with duffel bags."

"Exactly, but don't get too excited. There's no chance we get a warrant based on that."

"So, we take a closer look at the garage. And we have a lead."

"Yes to both." She clinked her cup against his. "To leads and smooth sailing. And here's the lab calling," Jordan added when her cell phone started vibrating on the table. "Perfect timing."

⚓︎

Ellie and Maria had sought out Dr. Hoffman who confirmed that he saw Jenkins' once a year for a check-up. He had no idea about the hoarding, though he revealed that Jenkins had mentioned going through difficult times after his divorce. They had found out that the woman in the picture was Victoria Haley, Ronald Jenkins' ex-wife. Not Judy.

While Maria finished up the interview with the doctor, Ellie stepped outside on the sidewalk to call the other number from Jenkins' address book. The phone was answered after the second ring.

"Hello, this is Judy," an anxious voice said. She sounded oddly familiar. Ellie ignored the feeling and continued.

"This is Detective Ellie Harding. We found your name in the address book of a Mr. Ronald Jenkins. Could you tell me your last name?"

"Wait, what? The police? Did something happen to Ronald?"

"Would you please come to the station, so we could talk?"

Silence.

Did Ronald Jenkins have an affair? Did she know about his living conditions, or was that relationship a thing of the past as well?

"I guess I can do that." The woman didn't sound very convinced. "You asked for my last name. It's Lawrence."

"Ms. Lawrence. I'm sorry I didn't recognize your voice right away. I could send someone over...no, wait. How about I come get you, and I can drive you home once we're done? I promise you it won't take long."

"Okay, but you said...Ronald?"

"I'm afraid he was found dead by a neighbor." Judy Lawrence didn't need to know details. "I'm sorry that I had to call you. I'll be there as soon as I can."

"Thank you, Detective Harding."

Ellie ended the call, stunned at what she'd learned. *It's a small world.* Judy Lawrence, the woman who had survived a serial killer thanks to Jordan's quick intervention. Said intervention had come at a great cost.

Judy had briefly been on their radar again when a group admiring the man had targeted his surviving victims, but Ellie hadn't heard anything from her since. Like Jenkins, Judy rarely left her home. It was a surprise that she had so quickly agreed to come to the station—or perhaps more had changed in her life than Ellie was aware of.

"What happened?"

Maria had joined her in front of the office. Her concerned tone shook her out of the trip down memory lane.

"I found out who Judy is," she said. "You won't believe this. Judy Lawrence."

"That's...interesting," Maria responded. "To say the least."

"It is. I told her I'd pick her up and we talk at the station."

"You do that. We'll meet back there."

"Okay."

43

Ellie called Ms. Lawrence back to tell her she was on her way. Another surprise greeted her when she made it to the address: Judy was waiting for her outside, on the stairs leading to her front door. Her reaction must have shown, because Judy shrugged.

"I guess I know what you're thinking, but I got tired of hiding inside. It didn't do me any good."

Ellie gave her what she hoped was an encouraging smile. She was more than glad to stay on topic.

"Again, I'm sorry for springing this on you. I can get you a coffee when we're there...In fact, I could use one."

After being confronted with the smells and sights of the day, food had been farthest from her mind, though her empty stomach was making itself known now.

"I won't say no to that," Judy returned politely.

They arrived at the station minutes later, and Ellie found an empty briefing room where she got Judy settled in. She quickly went to get coffee and a snack and returned to her witness.

"There you go. So...How did you know Mr. Jenkins?"

"I actually never met him in person," Judy said. "I still considered him a friend, because we shared some things."

That left a lot open to interpretation. Ellie thought back to her earlier theory.

"Whatever's on your mind, it's probably not that. There was nothing weird going on. He was already divorced when we met online." She shook her head. "It's strange, right, that I would trust anyone online after everything...but that's what happens when you spend most of your life inside, you seek a connection somewhere else. Anyway, there was nothing dangerous about him. I found him in a forum for trauma patients. The psychological kind."

"He'd been the victim of a crime?"

Ellie remembered that Judy, and Lori Gleason, another woman who had escaped Darby's torture chamber, had created and worked together in an advocacy group. Gleason had continued when Judy stepped away.

"Not in the same way, no. His family home burned to the ground. He never got over it, and eventually, the strain on the relationship was too much." Judy drank a sip of her coffee. "It's not the same, of course, but we could kind of relate in a way. Being angry at the world."

"You both had reason to be."

"No kidding. It just wasn't fair...random shit in his case, someone who didn't like the way I lived, in mine. We talked on a fairly regular basis, even after I met Shawn. My boyfriend," she clarified. "Before you go down that road, he knew all about Ronald, why I was talking to him and what about. He's not the jealous type. I wouldn't fall for that again."

Ellie wasn't yet sure she'd take her word for it. She made a mental note, hoping that Judy was right. If she had found love, great.

"Did you know Ronald was a hoarder?"

"We touched on that briefly. He didn't like to talk about it, as you can imagine. He was ashamed, but I guess he could open up to me a little bit, because I spent a lot of time inside with the curtains closed. He actually encouraged me to seek more help. I so wish he'd done the same." She wiped a tear from her eye, but more followed. "Excuse me."

Ellie found a box of tissues on one of the filing cabinets and handed it to her.

"There's no need. I'm really sorry...but I have to ask. Are you aware of anyone who might have wanted to do him harm?"

"Absolutely not. He was always polite, and kind." She sniffed and swallowed. "Damn, I swore to myself I wouldn't fall apart."

"You're doing great, Judy," Ellie told her softly. "Please, take your time."

"I wish I could help you. I just can't imagine...After his divorce, he cut ties with his family and friends, and he'd been living like that for years. One of his neighbors brought over food for him sometimes, but he wasn't close to them. I hate that things ended like this for him. He was a caring and intelligent man. He could talk numismatics for hours, and sometimes we did."

"Coins?" Ellie had to make sure she'd understood correctly. "He was a collector too?" They hadn't found anything related to the subject in the house, but there were still a lot of papers and junk to go through.

"For sure he wouldn't go to any conventions, then again, neither did I. He did continue to grow his collection. There's a lot you can find online."

Judy, however, hadn't been suffocating in clutter. Still, Ellie was fairly certain this detail was important.

"Do you know if he owned any rare coins?"

"I'm not sure. It's always been a hobby for me. He was more into it. In fact, his enthusiasm got me into collecting again. He did talk about a recent delivery, but I don't know what exactly it entailed. You think..."

"It's too early to tell if it's related, but we'll look into it. This has been very helpful. Thank you, Judy. I know it wasn't easy for you."

"I'm sad for Ronald," she admitted. "I'm actually doing better these days. He had a lot to do with that."

"I'll drive you home," Ellie offered.

"Thank you, but I don't think that's necessary. I'll call Shawn. He'll pick me up."

"If you prefer that, sure."

Two birds with one stone, so to speak, if she could get a glimpse at the boyfriend. Just in case.

Chapter Seven

On the surface, nothing suggested that Quentin had lied to them. He had started his business some seven years ago, and currently employed six mechanics. Sara and an intern who worked with her, plus his secretary. Business seemed to be booming. Jordan was a little less enthusiastic about the prospects when A.D.A. Esposito confirmed what she already knew.

"I'm really sorry, but I can't get you a warrant on a hunch."

"Don't be, I expected that," she said with a sigh.

"Any sign of the rest of the body?"

"No. The area is still being turned upside down, nothing yet. But I wish I knew what was in those duffel bags."

Valerie's eyes widened.

"Come on, no. I didn't think body parts. More like guns, rope, and duct tape?"

"Well, if you have anything, you'll know where to find me. I'm going to find my girlfriend and figure out if I have to eat dinner alone."

Jordan cast a look at Ellie's empty desk. Neither she nor Maria were anywhere to be seen.

"I guess they're still busy with the new case. Either way, have a good evening."

"Thanks."

Valerie Esposito left at the same time Lieutenant Daniels arrived. Jordan noticed that Derek hunched a bit behind his computer.

"Detective Henderson," Daniels said with a smile. "If you could come see me in my office? I believe there's also some development regarding your case?"

"Yes, Ma'am."

The doors opened again, but it wasn't Maria or Ellie, but Officer Libby Marshall, a man in his mid-forties with her.

⁂

The boyfriend had made it easy on Ellie, texting Judy that he was going to meet her inside. She and Judy had just left the briefing room. Ellie saw Officer Marshall with a man she assumed to be Shawn. Judy walked towards him but stopped in her tracks when she saw Jordan.

"Detective Carpenter, hi. I was wondering if I might see you here."

"Judy, hi. How are you?"

Jordan's tone and smile were polite. Ellie didn't think she was imagining the hint of reservation.

"I'm good, thank you," Judy answered, unaware. "And don't worry. It looks like I could help the police with a bit of my questionable expertise. Oh. I want you to meet my boyfriend Shawn," she said, before waving him over. "Shawn, this is Detective Carpenter."

Ellie stepped back a bit, watching as he shook hands with Jordan. Apparently, he didn't need more of an introduction.

"You're the one who saved Judy's life! Thank you so much," he said, seeming awe-struck.

"It's nice to meet you, Shawn."

"You too. When Judy asked me to pick her up, I had no idea it would be from a police station," he said, a half-hearted attempt at a joke.

Silence ensued, and before it could become too awkward, Ellie intervened. "Please, if you need anything, just call. Have a good evening."

Officer Marshall saw the couple out. Ellie noticed the thoughtful glance Jordan cast after them.

"I think this is a situation that requires more coffee."

Turning to her, Jordan said, "No kidding. Let's go."

***

In the break room, Jordan sat, leaning against the back of the chair. It wasn't that she needed more caffeine so badly, but the warmth was a much-needed comfort. Judy Lawrence, the coin collector. Her coins had been a killer's trophy.

"I know this was a surprise, but I don't think you, or Judy, for that matter, have to worry about anything. She's a hobby collector. My guy, Ronald Jenkins, was more serious about it. He likely owned more some more valuable coins, and someone found out about it."

Ellie sat across from her. "How's it going on your side?"

"Okay. Derek is inside with Daniels, and I don't think it's just about updating her. A vague lead so far. So, Judy has a boyfriend now."

"Yeah. According to what she says, it's the real thing."

Jordan detected a hint of doubt in Ellie's tone.

"But?"

"I wish there wasn't one," Ellie said with a sigh. "But I want to take a look at him, to be on the safe side. She spent a lot of time talking online to my victim...says Shawn wasn't jealous, but I want to be sure. She deserves to have a life, and love, after all this."

Jordan sensed there was a bit of a double meaning to those words.

"Yeah, she does. Let's make sure no one's trying to take advantage. At least, you will," she corrected herself. "I'll have to figure out if my idea has some merit, or if those co-workers at Quentin's were all best of friends."

"Good luck," Ellie said. "There's still a media blackout on the severed hand?"

"As long as that can last, yes. I'll have to get back to that as well."

Before leaving the room, they shared a quick kiss, knowing that it would be some time before they'd get home.

They took their coffees with them.

"I have a Mr. Clarkson here," Libby Marshall said apologetically. "He wants to talk to the investigator in charge of the scene at the amusement park."

Jordan had seen the name on a placard announcing the new building. The warrant had been served to the company, so her only surprise was that it didn't take them longer to get back to them.

She followed the officer into the waiting area where the man waiting there jumped to his feet. "What the hell are you doing on my construction site? A search I can understand, but you're opening up the ground?"

"Mr. Clarkson. Please come with me." Just as well. She didn't care much for thinking about Judy's visit, and what it might mean, at the moment. She asked him to sit in the visitor's chair and sat behind her desk. "We're sorry for the inconvenience, but it can't be avoided."

"Why? Was there a dead body on the premises?"

Jordan voiced her response carefully. "We have reason to believe that, yes. This is why we can't let you start the project until we have processed the scene."

The truth was, they still had no idea what happened to Randy Fowler's body. Someone like Clarkson was bound to have friends in high places and complain to them when things didn't go his way.

"Please understand that we are proceeding as quickly as we can. You'll be notified when the search is completed."

"You better. I'm losing a lot of money meanwhile. It's bad enough that some people are joking about the place being haunted. I don't need any more aggravation."

While unlikely to be haunted, Jordan had not found the grounds pleasant surroundings. She still had a hard time understanding what attracted Todd and Randy to them.

"You don't believe that crap?" he asked. "Clowns haunting the city, you'd think the police have more important things to do."

"Don't worry, we're not chasing after ghosts," she assured him. "We'll give you a call as soon as we're ready to move out."

He gave an exaggerated sigh. "Thank you, I guess."

"You're welcome, but thanks for stopping by so we could clear this up." She got up to see him out. "Just curious, those people saying the place is haunted—is there anyone in particular? Anyone who threatened you or might begrudge you the project?"

Mr. Clarkson looked fairly surprised at that.

"We've been working towards this moment for years. Sure, we got negative feedback, comments, over time. The latest ones were on social media, but I didn't take them seriously. With the holiday coming up...Some people want to be clever."

"You might be right. I'd still like you to save them and send me a link or a screenshot the next time." She handed him a business card.

She wasn't yet sure how a murder, a group of clowns, and this project could be connected, but she had the feeling they might be.

Talk about odd connections, the victim of Ellie's case being a friend of Judy Lawrence's.

The motive, in both cases, remained a mystery so far.

⁂

As it happened more often than they'd like, their daughter was sound asleep when they arrived home. Pauline Carpenter was on babysitting duty tonight. Not only had she tucked Meri in but also brought them food from the bar she and her husband Jack ran.

Jordan hugged her closely before she drove home.

"We'd be hopeless without you."

"Oh no, I don't think so, but I'm happy to make sure you're eating well."

Jordan had to admit she had a point.

"Can't argue with that. Thank you for everything—again."

"You're welcome. Will we see you this weekend? Jack won't be at the bar."

"I'll call you," Jordan promised. After she'd closed the door, her cell phone rang. With a bit of a guilty conscience, she let it go to voicemail. If it was urgent, she'd call Kathryn back. Jordan and her biological mother had made good progress towards reconciliation, but with everything the day had brought, she was not in the mood.

After a quick shower, she and Ellie sat down for dinner and the news afterwards, almost falling asleep on the couch.

Jordan woke with her heart racing, though she didn't remember any dreams. Ellie looked blissfully relaxed in sleep.

Jordan got out of bed and snuck into Meri's room. She wished she could go back to the same restful sleep that her wife and daughter were having, but she already knew it wasn't going to happen, too much on her mind. Not Darby, not really, she had learned not to give him that much importance. It was odd, though, the clown story turning from a prank to a vicious crime, the murdered hoarder, Judy, her boyfriend Shawn.

Not that those were related. She had enough on her plate trying to explain how the group—if they were the same—had gone from scaring people to dismembering Randy Fowler. She'd have to go back to Randy's grandmother, and Todd. She didn't look forward to either task. With a sigh, she turned away, intent on trying to get some rest.

Before going back to the bedroom, she went down to the kitchen to pour herself a glass of water. Still lost in thought, she jumped when she became aware of movement behind her.

"Just me," Ellie said softly. "I guess I came for the same reason."

"I'm good," Jordan felt the need to pre-empt any questions. She took another glass out of the cabinet and filled it for Ellie. "I just can't seem to figure this out. Why cut off someone's hand? There's a symbolism in that. I hate to even say that. I don't want another serial."

"It might be something else, even with the symbolism," Ellie suggested. "Retaliation. A warning to the other guy for whatever reason."

"According to Randy's grandma and boss, they were good boys. Hard-working."

"With connections somewhere to get cocaine."

"You're good."

Ellie smiled. "I know."

"And it's not even your case. You're not supposed to help, right? It's against the rules."

"I don't think that was what Daniels was talking about, but to be honest, I am no further on my case. So far, Shawn seems an okay guy. Maria found the ex-wife, but she and the daughter live two states away. They moved back to her hometown after the divorce. Jenkins is another good guy with no enemies."

"There's got to be something else."

"Yeah, but we're not going to find it tonight."

"Unfortunately you're right." Jordan placed their glasses in the sink. "Let's go back to bed."

They settled back under the sheets, Ellie fitting herself against her back, warm and comforting. For a few hours, she'd have to let the mysteries go. All of them.

Chapter Eight

The next morning, Daniels and Carroll were both present. They had called a meeting with all investigators to hear updates on their respective cases.

"We know that the hand definitely belonged to Randy Fowler," Jordan started.

"Is there any chance he could still be alive?" Daniels said.

"Not according to our medical examiner," Derek returned. "The hand was removed postmortem."

"Okay. But they let Williams go, didn't they? Do we know why, what set him apart?"

"We're not entirely sure. As of today, he still doesn't remember anything after running from the clowns." It unnerved her that she had to repeat the word. If anything, it showed her that their enthusiasm had been a tad premature. They didn't have all that much. Not one suspect.

"It is a good idea to talk to him again. Derek and I will go after the meeting. Maybe something will jog his memory."

"Let's hope," Carroll commented. "Detectives Doss, Harding?"

"Yes," Ellie said quickly. "We're still looking, but thanks to Ms. Lawrence we know that Mr. Jenkins was a collector of rare coins. He expected a package. If someone knew about it, they might have tried to get their hands on it."

"Chances are they didn't find what they were looking for. If Jenkins didn't tell them…Where would anyone start?" Maria shrugged. "It was hard to even recognize a struggle, or if someone had been searching for something. That place was stuffed to the ceiling. We're still trying to figure out if anything was stolen—and the ex-wife wasn't of any help."

"You keep looking. What about the connection to Judy Lawrence?"

Ellie cast a quick look at Jordan before she answered.

"They never met in person, but they'd been talking online for some time. They connected in a chat room for trauma survivors. He lost his home in a fire."

"Did anyone get hurt in the fire?" Jordan asked.

"No, but they lost everything. Had to stay in a shelter for a while, because neither of them had relatives close by. They filed for divorce the same year. No motive yet, but we're also looking at his online profile, someone he might have told about the coin—or coins—he was expecting, or if he got into an argument with someone."

Carroll looked a bit pained, probably thinking of the red tape they'd need to cut through to get to that other person, if they existed.

"All right. Thank you, everyone. Now, let's get back to work."

On the way to the hospital, Jordan was still pondering the different angles discussed in the meeting. She kept coming back to one particular point.

"I hate this," she said with emphasis. "How messed up is this, cutting off someone's hand? If they wanted to send a message, I don't see anyone getting it, us, or the person it's directed at."

"Maybe Todd didn't tell us everything," Derek suggested. "If we can jog his memory, he might fill in some of the blanks for us. Except if he has something to hide."

"You think someone threatened him?"

"Not exactly."

Taking a guess, Jordan returned, "No, I think those two were solid. That doesn't mean he told us everything he knows."

"What about the contractor? Did he get back to you?" Derek asked.

"Not yet, but that's vague too." Jordan suppressed a yawn.

"Meri keeping you up?"

"The case is keeping me up," she said. "Clowns. This is ridiculous, but a man is dead, and I want to know why."

"We'll figure it out."

Jordan hoped he was right.

Ellie was lost in thought when she sat at her desk, waiting for Chris Atwood whom she'd sent to get more of the boxes from Jenkins' house. To her surprise and relief, he hadn't questioned her or talked back to her. Perhaps Sergeant Bristol had had a stern word with him.

"Wow, hey, look at this!"

"For Christ's sake!" Her reaction was a bit stronger than she'd intended.

Atwood lowered the mask encased in an evidence bag and set down the box.

"There's a lot more where this came from, but I need another hand if you want it all at your desk," he said, placing the mask on top of the desk. "It was in there. Geez. Sorry."

"Forget about it." She'd had reason to be stunned simply to hear Atwood apologize, but Ellie had no time for any of it. "This is from Mr. Jenkins' house?" she asked.

"Yes, what you asked me to get. But there are a ton more of those. Boxes, I mean. Save for the computer, that's still with the lab."

Maria had gone to talk to Anna Crawford, head of the lab, for the phone records and any findings on Ronald Jenkins' computer.

"Okay. Thank you. Yes, I still want all of it. Get a couple of guys to help you."

She picked up the item and headed for Lieutenant Carroll's office where she knocked on the door.

"Come in."

His eyes widened when he saw what she was holding in her hand.

"Harding, please tell me this is something good."

"Lieutenant, this was found among Jenkins' things. I was going to get it to the lab ASAP, but I just wanted to let you know."

"Thanks. If that wasn't Jenkins', and he doesn't seem like the type who liked to host costume parties…What are the odds that there's a connection?"

Ellie cast a look at the clown's mask. "To the clown sightings, the murders, or both," she mused.

"This is just getting worse," he said. "Let me know what you find out."

"Yes, sir."

When he noticed Ellie's hesitation, he asked, "Is there anything else?"

She almost denied it, given the urgency of the situation.

"I was wondering if we should expect any more changes…transfers and such. I know now's not the time, but…"

"These past weeks have been difficult," he acknowledged. "I made sure that all of your jobs are safe. I made it a condition."

Ellie wasn't sure what to say. Finally, she settled on "Thank you, sir. We appreciate it."

"Daniels will bring some new ideas, and they're good ones. I hope you'll give her a chance."

"We will, and thank you again. Now I think I should..." She held up the bag, and he nodded.

Their trip to the hospital was in vain as Todd Williams had been discharged earlier. Making a detour to his address, Jordan and Derek found him at home on his couch. Lisa was home as well, making lunch in the kitchen. She had seen them into the small living room. The surroundings were tidy but cramped.

"Hey," Todd said. "You have any news on Randy?"

"I'm afraid so," Derek told him.

Todd listened to him relating the recent events, all but screeching in the midst of it,

"They cut off his hands?"

"Hand," Derek corrected. "But it was done afterwards. You told us you heard a gunshot that night. Did anything else come back to you?"

"Not really," Todd answered him. "Wow, that's...Who would do something like that?"

"That's what we're trying to find out. Did Randy ever mention having trouble with anyone, at work maybe?"

Todd shook his head. "No way, those guys were tight. They didn't even make fun of him for living with his grandma...not that there's anything to make fun of, but you know how guys can be."

Jordan made a non-committal sound. It seemed to her that not making fun of someone for their living conditions was setting the bar fairly low.

"One of the customers though, now that you mention it. He brought in a car that was all messed up, then pretended it was Randy's fault. Yeah, I remember that. But this was a stuck-up guy in a suit. I don't see how he would dress up as a clown, let alone cut off somebody's hand." He shuddered.

Jordan noticed Lisa standing in the doorway. She looked like she was about to get sick.

"Perhaps we should cut this short," she said. "Todd isn't feeling so well yet."

"We are almost done," Jordan assured her. "Todd, this was a one-time thing, or did he come back?"

"I don't know. He mentioned him once. And the pretty girlfriend, or wife. She seemed embarrassed."

Derek's cell phone rang. He excused himself and stepped outside the room, only to return a moment later. "Thank you very much, Mr. Williams, Ms. Garner. This is all for now. Jordan?"

Outside the door he said, "Take a look at this. Ellie found this among the coin collector's things."

"All right, that's interesting. Perhaps we can talk about it during lunch? I'd still like to swing by the garage. First, we should go back in there."

Lisa opened the door to them once more, a hint of irritation showing on her face.

"Is there anything else?"

They followed her into the kitchen, where the table was set for two. Todd Williams sat in one of the chairs.

"This won't take long. Todd, can you tell us if you've seen this before?"

"Whoa." He recoiled from the image. "I'm about to start eating."

Jordan exchanged a look with Derek. Was his reaction a bit overly dramatic? Then again, they still didn't know the exact details of his experience.

"I'm sorry about that. So...?"

"Could be one of them. I'm not sure." He shrugged. "They sell them everywhere right now. It's hard to tell."

At least he wasn't ruling it out. His answer wasn't helping much either.

"That's all for now. Thank you, Todd. Lisa."

⁂

This time, they came into the building through the back of the garage. A couple of mechanics were working on a jacked-up vehicle.

"I'm sorry, but you need to go in through reception," one of them said.

Jordan showed him her badge and introduced herself and Derek. "I think we're good. We're here about Randy Fowler..."

"And I told you, you can come to me with any questions," Mr. Quentin said behind them. "No need to keep these guys from doing their work. They don't know anything."

"We would like to talk to all your employees," Jordan returned. "We've been told that a customer recently harassed Randy, even threatened to sue him. We'd like to find that customer."

"Really, who told you that? I can't remember Randy having any trouble, ever. And for sure I'd know if someone wanted to sue one of my employees. Guys, did you hear anything?"

Both of them shook their heads.

"See, problem solved." Mr. Quentin acted a bit cheerful for someone whose employee had been *murdered*. "Is there anything else I can help you with?"

"Perhaps reception met that customer?"

There was a hint of impatience in the man's voice when he said, "You'd be wasting your time, but by all means, go ahead."

Sara, the receptionist, confirmed that she'd never heard about the mysterious customer while Quentin kept hovering.

"It's a shame about Randy," she said. "Such a bright young man."

"He supposedly came in the week before Randy disappeared. Could we take a look at your records?"

"I'm sorry, Detective, but we all know that unless you have a warrant, those records are confidential. I swear to you, they wouldn't help you anyway. There was no such client."

"All right. Thank you."

Back in the car, Jordan was about to call Ellie when a text message came in. She realized with a somewhat guilty conscience that she'd never called Kathryn back. Suppressing a sigh, she decided the moment was as good as any.

Kathryn picked up right away.

"Jordan. I'm so glad you called."

"I don't have much time..." That, still, seemed to be her standard greeting. "How are you?"

"Okay," Kathryn said quickly. "We're good."

"So..."

"I just wanted to know if you wanted to come over for dinner sometime, bring Meri...You haven't been over since Jim and I moved into the apartment."

"True. Look, I'll have to call you back. We're pretty busy right now, but I'll look at our schedules and get back to you."

"Don't take too long."

"What do you mean?"

Kathryn laughed nervously. "Oh, you know, figure of speech. You never know, right? I'd just love to see you."

"Sure. I'll let you know soon. That was weird," Jordan said after she'd ended the call. Derek didn't comment. "Then again, it's always going to be a bit weird. No need to drop everything and go see her."

"You decide. If you'd like to use lunch time…"

"No. She wanted us to come over for dinner. I don't think it's urgent."

"Your call," Derek said with a shrug.

"Right. Speaking of calls, I should let Ellie and Maria know where to meet. How about the station? I have a sudden craving for pizza. We could pick it up on the way."

"You having a craving for pizza is never sudden or unexpected." He laughed. "All right, let's do it."

Chapter Nine

Typing the numbers of Judy Lawrence's phone number, Ellie watched as a couple of delivery men brought two desks into the room. It was already a fairly tight fit whenever everyone was present. This could be a challenge, but at least they'd have additional staff. Across the city and county, not all units had faired this well.

"This is Judy's phone?"

She recognized Shawn's voice. "Shawn, hi, this is Detective Harding, we met yesterday. Is Judy anywhere near?"

"Yes, of course, just a moment."

On the other end, she heard what sounded like footsteps, and a knocking sound. Muted voices, then Judy was on the line.

"Detective. What's the matter?"

"Hello Judy. How are you?"

"You didn't call to ask me that?" She laughed a little. "Sorry about that. I'm doing okay."

"Good. This might sound strange to you, but I have to ask. In recent conversations with Mr. Jenkins or anyone—or at all—did anyone ever bring up clowns?" Ellie cringed at her line of questioning.

"It's strange that you should ask that," she said. "Actually...He once said that there was someone in a mask walking by his window. It creeped me out a bit."

"He didn't report it?"

"We thought it was just some kid taking themselves and the holiday too seriously. I mean, look at all the fake dead bodies and zombies on front lawns. Besides, you saw his house. He wasn't so sure anyone would have thought it was serious, I guess."

"I'm so sorry," Ellie said.

"Can I ask why now? You know who killed him?"

"Not yet, but thank you, Judy."

"You're welcome...Come on, give me a couple of minutes here? Not you, Detective. I'm sorry, I have to go."

The delivery men had finished setting up the desks and were about to leave. An incoming text message startled Ellie out of disturbing thoughts about clowns sneaking around Jenkins' house, and the true nature of Judy and Shawn's relationship.

She got up and went to find Maria, suppressing a yelp when she bumped her hip into one of the new desks.

This would take some time getting used to.

"Jenkins' online history is eighty percent about coins, and the rest is delivery of food and clothes. Communication, mostly the trauma group, almost all of it Judy Lawrence," Maria said once they had joined Jordan and Derek and set up lunch in the break room. "About those coins, I don't understand a lot. You said Lawrence was an expert?"

"She called it a hobby," Ellie corrected, "but if we need an expert, I guess she could help us with that." She was still worried that Jordan's insomnia might have to do with Judy's relation to hers and Maria's case. Which now seemed related to the clown case, unless various groups of men had decided to give committing crimes in the costume a go. Taking a look at the slice of pizza on her plate, she sighed. "Green peppers?"

"I'll have them," Jordan offered. "Sorry. I asked them not to put any but didn't check if they got it right."

Ellie ignored the indulgent gaze Maria and Derek shared when Jordan picked the offending toppings off her slice. "And he did see a person with a clown mask. He didn't think it was necessary to bring it to the police."

"That's so cute," Maria commented.

"Funny." Jordan continued where Ellie had left off. "I still think Quentin and his crew are hiding something. But there's still nothing to connect them to Jenkins other than that mask. And no real motive." Jordan sounded frustrated.

"Look on the bright side," Maria offered. "If we get this done before Halloween, perhaps Ellie's friend can make it a big story. But really? Who doesn't like peppers on their pizza?"

Ellie shrugged to both. "Me, that's who." As for the potential story...Jill Allen, a reporter and friend, had warned them about upcoming changes at the department early on, and she trusted her. But for her to write a sympathetic one, they had to give her results.

"I think the new detectives are coming soon. They brought the desks in earlier," she said.

"New desks? That's a good thing," Derek said. "I was afraid I'd have to share with my messy partner here." That brought him laughs all around, except from Jordan who scowled at him.

"I'm not messy. Just not as OCD as you are. And yes, I'm glad we don't have to share too."

"Back to the matter at hand." Ellie shuddered a little realizing that the term hit a bit close to home. "We'll have to wait for the lab results on that mask. Meanwhile, I'm still not sure about Shawn."

"Is it a hunch, or do you have reason?" Maria asked. Ellie noticed that Jordan sat up straighter, leaning in a fraction.

"A hunch for now," she admitted. "They seemed to have a bit of an argument when we were on the phone earlier, but of course that doesn't have to mean anything. There's no reason she can't be happy and in love after...what happened."

No one disagreed with her.

Something still bothered Ellie.

"Good, you're all here. Meet Detectives Wu and Murphy," Lieutenant Daniels said, Carroll standing by her side. "They're arriving with their own caseload for now, but in the future, we'll shift to cases coming in."

After a round of introductions and handshakes, Maria and Ellie went back to sorting through some more of Ronald Jenkins' belongings. Finally, a box that held a few coins still in packaging. They looked recent, and new, not the kind someone would get a huge amount of money, let alone kill for. A couple of empty packages.

Ellie looked over to Jordan's desk and suppressed a smile when she realized Derek had a point. Of course, brought together, their differing methods had led them to hold a record in this unit, something to aspire to. Wu and Murphy were in the lieutenant's office. She went back to her sheet of paper and wrote down, *Scared child, near accident, woman in parking garage.*

Kidnapping. Murder. Could they have prevented this escalation? She wasn't sure how, or what made Jenkins, Fowler, and Williams different from those who were only victims of pranks that might have gone bad.

Specifically, a connection between the ones who were murdered.

Were they right to look at Jenkins' passion for numismatics? Did the murderer even know?

❧

Earlier that day, Pauline and Jack had taken Meri to their own house. After their shift, Jordan and Ellie went over to the *SEVEN* to have dinner and pick up their daughter.

The place was decorated for Halloween, though in an understated, tame way.

"Two evening specials, and one happy baby for you," Jack joked when he handed his granddaughter to Jordan. "You're coming in at a reasonable time. That's got to be a good sign."

"Not much of a sign," Jordan admitted after kissing Meri's cheek. "Things are moving. I'd prefer if they were moving quicker."

"One evening special…and here's my Goddaughter."

Meri made excited sounds in Derek's direction, but Jordan shook her head. "No way. I haven't seen her all day. You get in line."

One by one, their friends assembled in the private room they often used now when Meri was here.

"Is it bad that we didn't invite the new guys?" Maria wondered out loud.

"No," Derek said. "After the latest scandal, they of all people will understand why we take our time."

No one needed any further explanation. Murphy and Wu had worked more closely with Shriver, the detective who had tried hard to make friends in Homicide…and then committed two.

If anything, everyone wanted to focus on the job and move on.

It was likely the same for the new additions to their unit.

Another night, the same procedure. Jordan scowled at her mirror image. All things considered, she was doing fine, and the occasional nightmare wasn't enough to prove otherwise. She could have done without them too.

The funhouse, the locked door, and the man with a clown's mask in the mirror.

Was that the last thing Randy had seen?

Ronald Jenkins?

Todd, before he was dragged off to someplace still unknown?

She would have loved to search Quentin's offices and private residence, but that remained a pipe dream as long as they didn't have solid evidence. It was no surprise that even in sleep, her brain mulled over the questions. She was somewhat surprised to find the man behind the mask had been Noah Shriver. She'd never felt like it was his intent to do her harm. If anything, his actions had been more suicidal. He was serving a prison sentence.

She wondered how he'd feel about two of his colleagues now teaming up with Homicide, for a more or less political reason. He'd wanted to force things. What goes around comes around.

This time, she managed to sneak back into bed without waking Ellie. Shriver might not have wanted to hurt her, but there was no saying what could have happened that night. She carefully snuggled against her back, once again comforted by the closeness. Those dreams weren't about her own experiences so much as they were about fearing for the ones she loved. And that was as irrational as anything, because there was no direct threat to them, only a bunch of murdering clowns they needed to get off the streets. And they would.

Chapter Ten

E llie had done a bit of her own research on the sets of coins
they had found at Jenkins'. The value of some of them had
risen since their purchase, but nothing dramatic so far. Nothing
to justify bothering Judy again.

She went back to the transcripts they had of Judy's conversations with him. With only hints at the trauma each of them
had faced, most of the communications were about precious
pennies, luster composition and finish. Judy didn't own riches.
When Darby had taken some of her coins, it wasn't for the
monetary value, but because this hobby represented something
uniquely about her.

But this wasn't about him. He was dead and buried. Ellie hated the idea that anything of the present cases—or case—might
trace back to him or his fan club. To her relief, it didn't look like
they had to go down that road, but it was hard to ignore the
context completely.

She shifted and winced, reminded of the bruise she'd gotten
earlier running into one of the new desks. She noticed the new
detectives talking to each other.

The sound of rapid footsteps made her look up. Carroll was
coming out of his office with Daniels in tow.

"Listen," he said in a stern tone. "We've had another clown sighting, witness says they seemed to carry something heavy. I need everyone on this."

The witness had stopped at the restaurant a couple of miles from where she'd encountered the alarming sight, and they met her there.

"I was driving by. I could see them walking in that direction...One of them looked right at me. I was afraid they might get my license plate. With my son in the car, I didn't want to take the risk." The woman held a boy of about two years old in her arms.

Jordan could sympathize. "You did the right thing."

"You don't think it's silly?"

"No, not at all. My colleagues and I will take it from here. Thank you. Will you be okay to drive home?"

"I'm fine," she said.

It looked nothing but random. Jordan had to make sure. "Has anyone bothered you recently?"

"No. I read about those clowns popping up and scaring people. I thought I'd better call before anyone gets hurt."

"That was the right decision," Jordan assured her once more. "Thank you."

She went back to find Derek, Maria and Ellie who were about to start searching the nearby woods along with the uniformed officers on the scene.

When they started out, Ellie could still see Libby to her left, and Derek to the right. As they ventured deeper into the forest, voices got more muted, and it grew quiet around her. Before long, she didn't see anyone.

She had been to these woods a couple of times as a uniformed officer, first, when they were looking for a child who had run away from her would-be kidnapper, then, during the chase for escaped felon Phil Hobbs.

It seemed like every time she set foot in them, it was dark and dreary, always fitting for the occasion.

She'd been the one to find the girl.

Hobbs' flight had ended eventually.

Somehow, she was convinced that this case would be more complicated. These men—likely—were mocking their victims, and the police. They might have known that Jenkins would be hesitant to contact the authorities.

Jordan had hinted that she believed Todd Williams was keeping secrets from them.

What made these damn clowns so powerful...and elusive?

She made sure to pay close attention to any possible hint of another person. They could only hope that the group's destination had been somewhere in these woods, and that nothing had tipped them off yet. If they had a car waiting close by, the police might be too late.

She thought about the witness claiming they'd carried something heavy. Did that mean they were moving Randy Fowler's body? Why?

Worse, was there another victim?

She bent down to pick up a cigarette butt, noticing a hint of something red. Lipstick. Walking further, she barely avoided stumbling over tree roots, pausing for a second to catch her breath.

As she looked around, careful not to miss anything important, her gaze fell on something flashy hidden in the shrubs. Ellie crouched down to take a closer look, realizing she was looking at the strap of a woman's purse.

"Hello? Is anybody there?" Given the past few days, she felt disheartened enough to assume she might stumble over another dead body rather than a living person. She paused again, trying to make out any sounds that weren't the leaves in the wind or the voices of her colleagues from afar.

Then she found it.

Ellie sped up her pace, the purse still with her in a plastic bag when she came to the tree in a denser area of the wood.

"Oh my God. Give me a moment, I'll get you out of here. I'm with the police."

She hadn't met the woman, but Ellie knew who she was from the picture she'd seen on Jordan's desk—Lisa Garner, Todd Williams' girlfriend. She looked to be freezing, only wearing jeans and a t-shirt, socks but no shoes.

Another piece of the puzzle, though Ellie wasn't wasting any time. She tested the knots of the rope binding Lisa to the tree, noting that the material had already broken skin.

"I'm so sorry. It will only take a moment, then we'll get you to the hospital." She spoke softly, aware of the woman's teeth chattering. Ellie started to peel away the duct tape over her lips. "You'll be okay."

Lisa Garner's eyes widened dramatically, and for a split-second, Ellie misinterpreted the sign. "I know this is going to hurt for a second, but we want to get this off, right?"

There was a minute change in the air behind her, before a sharp pain at the base of her skull distracted her from the task at hand.

When she opened her eyes, her vision was blurry. She must have been out for a moment. How long, Ellie wasn't sure, but looking around, she realized Lisa was gone.

"I need some help here!"

She tried to get up using the nearest tree. Her head started to spin and her surroundings went dark once again.

❦

Jordan had not seen anything but trees and branches until Libby Marshall came sprinting towards her.

"I need you to come with me."

"What happened?"

"I called an ambulance already," Libby rasped. "Ellie...She was knocked out. She's conscious now, and Wes is with her—"

Jordan didn't need to hear anything else.

"Wait here for the ambulance," she told Derek who had joined them, and hasted to follow Libby back into the direction she had come from.

"I think I saw one of them from afar," the younger officer told her. "I had to make sure Ellie was okay first."

"Of course."

Everything happened in a matter of minutes, yet it seemed like an eternity before she got to crouch down beside Ellie who was sitting up on the damp ground about a mile away, holding her head. Cursing.

Jordan suppressed a smile. That had to be a good thing, right?

"Hey. What happened?" Touching the back of Ellie's head, alarm gripped her when her fingers came away wet. "You shouldn't be moving."

"I'm not moving much," Ellie said, her voice sounding apprehensive. "And...wow, this hurts."

"Are you going to be sick?"

"No, I don't think so."

Jordan wasn't entirely convinced. She shrugged out of her coat and laid it out. "The ambulance will be here soon. You should lie down."

"You're getting your coat dirty for no reason. Lisa was here, and...damn, they took her, right?"

"Lisa?" Jordan went with the obvious question first. She wasn't sure what to make of the other, alarmed to find Ellie sounding confused. "Let's get you checked out first."

"Yes, Lisa Garner. She was here, tied to the tree. Damn it. I should have gotten her free before they returned. They're going to kill her too."

"Who's they?"

Ellie paused for a few seconds, then she shook her head in frustration. "I can't tell you. Everything happened so fast. But it must have been the clowns, right? Libby? Did you see them?"

Officer Marshall stepped closer, her expression apologetic. "Just one of them, I think. They were wearing dark clothes, but too far for me to see anything else."

"You should have gone after them," Ellie muttered. "I'm okay!"

"We'll figure it out," Jordan assured her. "Let's take care of you now."

Fortunately, Derek arrived at this moment with two paramedics.

"You need to find Lisa," Ellie insisted. "She might know something. Maybe she saw them without masks. They can't have gotten that far."

"We'll take care of it," Derek said, addressing Jordan. "You can go."

"No. I'll be fine. I can walk." Ellie got to her feet only to sway dangerously, the two paramedics catching her and lowering her gently onto the gurney. She muttered another curse, but Jordan wasn't fooled.

"I'll follow the ambulance," she said.

"Jordan. Wait a second." She turned to Derek who pointed at the base of the tree. The rope almost blended in with the tree roots.

"Call in more back-up. I'll be back as soon as I can, see if Ellie remembers some more."

They both knew it wasn't the only reason.

"She'll be fine."

"Of course."

It would be ridiculous to suggest anything else.

Her priority at this moment was Ellie, so she had to push any worst-case scenarios aside and focus on driving. Meanwhile, the questions had multiplied. Why Lisa? According to Todd Williams, she didn't even know that he used to hang out at the amusement park with Randy Fowler. Jordan remembered her standing in the doorway the other day, eager to usher the cops out of her place. Because she was worried about Todd? Because she knew more than she'd let on? Or was it Todd who had put her in danger, unintentionally or for a reason he was well aware of?

They had to find her. Lisa might have the answers they needed to close two cases.

She parked the car in the hospital lot and then all but ran to the entrance. At the front desk, she asked the nurse about Ellie.

"Detective Harding. She was just brought in."

"The doctor is with her now. You can see her in a minute."

After receiving directions, Jordan was unwilling to wait any longer. She walked past the ER doors and found Ellie with a doctor at the back of the room.

She looked pale in the light of the lamps overhead, but she smiled.

"Hey. Any news on Lisa?"

"Not yet. Derek will call me the moment they find her. How are you?"

"Pissed. My head hurts."

"Which comes as no surprise," the doctor who had finished his exam, commented. "You have a concussion, Detective."

"Does she need to stay overnight?" Jordan asked.

Ellie made a face, but the doctor hurried to assure her.

"That won't be necessary. I'll give you anti-nausea medication, and the headache should go away with some Tylenol. You'll need rest, and I advise you to take a couple of days at least. If the headache persists, or if there are any of the other symptoms we've discussed, I'd like to see you back here ASAP."

"I can do that. Thanks," Ellie said.

"When you go back to work, be sure to take breaks and limit physical exertion. I'll go make sure that your release papers are ready."

When he was out of earshot, Ellie sighed in relief. "That's a good surprise in all of this. I was afraid they might be keeping me."

Jordan leaned in to softly kiss her temple. She, too, was grateful that this incident hadn't led to worse results.

"I'll drive you home."

"Thank you. But you don't need to stay. It's bad enough that one of us is useless while time is running out for Lisa."

"Now, come on, that's not your fault. You didn't choose to be hit over the head," Jordan reminded her. Her own mind was slow to calm down. She could handle nightmares and weird cases but seeing Ellie hurt had her on edge.

Chapter Eleven

During the drive home, Jordan wondered what the next few days would look like. Pauline, who was currently at Jordan and Ellie's home with Meri, could probably stay a bit longer. They'd be fine for today, and the weekend was coming up. So far, not so bad. Yet, Jordan still had a job to do.

"Like the doctor said, you should rest, but if you remember anything else, just call me, okay?"

"Oh no." Ellie made a frustrated sound.

"What is it?"

"I found a cigarette butt—and then, her purse, before I saw her. None of it was on me when I came in, was it?"

"I'll check, but I'm pretty sure they took her purse. The only thing left was a bit of rope on the ground."

"She was so scared," Ellie remembered. "I failed her."

That might be a bit dramatic, but given the situation, Jordan wasn't going to point it out.

"No one could have expected what happened. So, you found the cigarette, then the purse, which led you to Lisa. Did she say anything?"

With the same frustrated expression, Ellie shook her head.

"There was no time. I was about to remove the duct tape…" She winced, and Jordan didn't need any further explanation.

"Is there anything else?"

"No, sorry."

"It's fine. We'll find her."

Ellie nodded, but she didn't say anything. They both knew that with every passing minute, it was less likely they'd find her alive.

⁂

"You're early," Pauline remarked when they walked into the living room.

One of the many things Jordan admired about Pauline was that she always remained calm, no matter how worried she was, very different from her memories of her biological mother. Kathryn had changed a lot, but this striking difference still warranted a fleeting thought.

"Yes. Ellie has a concussion."

"A concussion! What happened?" Worry was shining through now, but she still kept her tone low and quiet.

Jordan did her best to summarize the events without too many frightening details.

"Doc says she'll be okay, but no matter what she says, she needs to rest."

"All right. I'll make sure of that," Pauline said, prompting Ellie to laugh wryly.

"Hey. I'm right here."

"We're aware, sweetie. Why don't you lie down? I can make you something to eat later, something easy on the stomach."

"In a minute." Ellie crouched down to kneel next to Meri who was playing on a blanket on the floor but happily abandoning her toys in exchange for hugs. Ellie picked her up, her smile mostly fueled by stubbornness, Jordan assumed. She wasn't fooled.

"I think the doctor was pretty clear. Rest first. Play with the baby after the pain pills kick in."

Her daughter's happy sounds were a huge distraction, but Jordan reminded herself that she had no excuse to stay. "If there's any nausea or vomiting, or the headache doesn't go away..."

"We'll get her to the hospital right away," Pauline promised.

"Okay. I guess I need to go back," Jordan said before she embraced both her wife and daughter, reluctantly stepping back. Her phone rang, another reminder of the task at hand. She waved to her family and answered the phone on the way back to the car.

"Carpenter."

"Hey, are you still at the hospital?" Derek asked.

"No, just leaving home. We were getting Ellie settled in."

"How is she?"

"Concussion. Doctor says she'll be fine."

"That's good. I want you to meet me back at the hospital. They're going to bring in Lisa Garner."

It wasn't hard to interpret the tone of his voice.

"How bad is it?" That question took priority over the others. When? How?

"I don't know the whole story yet. Bruises, exposure, she'll definitely need some care. And she's terrified."

"But lucid, talking? That means..."

"She might help us identify who kidnapped her and assaulted Ellie. I'll be right there with you."

***

Finally, a break. Lisa had to remember something. The idea of wrapping up this case soon appealed to Jordan as she walked along the same hallways once again, on her way to Lisa's room.

She curbed her enthusiasm when she stepped inside to talk to the traumatized young woman, softening her voice as she greeted her. Lisa looked younger, a lot more vulnerable than the last time she had seen her, the redness around her mouth and wrists reminders of her ordeal.

"Lisa, hi. I'm so sorry."

Lisa's eyes darted around as if she expected her attackers to be in the room. Jordan thought back to when they'd first talked to Todd Williams after his abduction, the similar mannerism. Not surprising for someone who had been held against their will. She felt the shiver winding its way down her spine. Coming to this place twice in one day made her antsy.

"Can you tell us what happened?" Jordan asked. At first, she wasn't sure the other woman had understood her. "Lisa?"

"I don't know," Lisa offered hesitantly.

"Who tied you to that tree?"

"I don't know, I swear! I finished my shift earlier today, went to my car and...Someone put a sack over my head. They had a knife. I was so scared!"

"That's understandable. Can you remember anything else? A smell, a sound? Did anyone speak to you?"

"No. I passed out...the next thing I knew I was in the woods. I tried to get loose, but I couldn't make it. Then the officer arrived. She tried to free me, but..."

"What happened then?" Jordan asked when Lisa didn't continue.

"I'm not sure."

"Lisa, this is serious," Derek said calmly. "Detective Harding was hurt. Someone hit her from behind while she was trying to free you. It would be incredibly helpful if you could describe them to us."

"But I can't! I...I don't remember."

Jordan was fairly sure of two things: Lisa Garner wasn't telling the truth. And she was scared out of her mind.

"I know you've been through a lot, with what happened to Todd, and now...But this is important. The people who took you, were they wearing masks? Do you know any of them?"

"I can't help you. I'm sorry. I don't remember anything after she found me."

"You might have been drugged," Derek acknowledged. "We'll find out after the tox screen."

"I didn't take anything intentionally," she said. "Not like Todd."

"We'll talk later," Jordan told her. "Unless there's anything else you want to share..."

"No. I'd like to be alone if you don't mind. Todd's on his way."

"Okay. Take good care."

She waited until they were in the hallway before giving voice to her frustration. "I'm glad she's okay, considering, but what the hell was that?"

"Beats me," Derek admitted. "We found her about a half hour after Ellie, crouching behind an old shed. She seems fairly lucid, but she can't or won't say what happened. Sounds strangely familiar."

"Like Todd. I get it that they're both traumatized, were possibly drugged, but I still think there's more to it. They are afraid, and unless they start talking, more people are going to get hurt."

"Looks like Ellie was lucky though."

"Yeah. They might have a real beef with Todd and Lisa. This...it seems like they want to mock us."

Derek didn't offer an alternative interpretation.

Ellie's headache was starting to abate, but the many worries on her mind were not, her thoughts going around in circles. Since she'd made detective, and joined the Homicide unit a few months afterwards, she'd had considerable successes. Today's events made her wonder if most of it was actually her work, or if it was just easy to shine next to Waters phoning it in.

They had answered to the call of a suspicious clown sighting, a group who had likely already killed two men. Could she have predicted any of it? Should she have been more careful?

All that was on her mind was to get those ropes and the duct tape off of the poor woman.

Her mind went back to her own case, Judy Lawrence, and finally, what Jordan had done to save her.

Should Ellie have called her colleagues first? Would that have made any difference?

She couldn't imagine it would have. But where had Lisa's, and probably Todd Williams' kidnappers gone? Disappeared into thin air like characters from a horror movie? She shuddered, then jumped when there was a soft knock on the door.

"I made you some soup," Pauline said. "I can warm it up later if you don't feel like it now..."

Ellie's first impulse was to refuse, but she'd already created more work for Jordan and Pauline. To her surprise, her stomach was making a faint sound at the mention of food.

"I should give it a try."

"Great. I'll bring you a bowl."

Shortly after Pauline left the bedroom, the phone rang. Pauline returned a few minutes later with a bowl of soup on a tray, and good news.

"That was Jordan," she said. "She wanted me to tell you that they found the woman."

Neither of them had expected tears. Ellie would chalk it all up to the head injury. At least the smell of the soup didn't make her nauseated—small favors.

⁂

There was no sign that Lisa had changed her mind. Jordan sat at her desk, but she wasn't getting much work done, her mind on how lives had been changed in a heartbeat. Randy, Todd, Lisa...

Ellie. It was unreal. She felt a cold shiver skitter down her spine, in spite of all the reassurances. Those clowns—she scowled at her own thought—what was their endgame? Mocking the police, sure, but this didn't look like a deliberate act. They hadn't targeted Ellie specifically. They'd tried to stop her from helping Lisa.

Who?

"Detective Carpenter. I'm sure that paperwork can wait until tomorrow." She looked up to see Lieutenant Daniels standing in front of her desk.

"I'm afraid you're right. Lisa's not talking, and the tox screen might not come in today."

"If it does, the night shift will be here."

"I could use some time," Jordan admitted. "My mother is helping out at home, but..."

"Then go. This..." She made a sweeping motion across the desk. "...will all be here tomorrow."

"True. Thank you."

Aware of Daniels' sober expression, Jordan waited.

"I'm glad you were able to rescue Ms. Garner. But this is exactly the situation I was trying to avoid. Tomorrow, I'd like you and Detective Henderson to fill in Detectives Wu and Murphy on the case. I'd like to reassign Detective Doss."

"Okay."

"This is not a punishment. Everyone did their jobs. But it looks more and more like the murders, Fowler and Jenkins, might somehow be related. I want to give Detective Harding enough time to recover. I don't want her out in the field before she's one hundred percent."

"I understand. The doctor said to take at least a couple of days."

"We'll see after the weekend. Let me know if you need anything."

"Thanks, Lieutenant. Good night."

⊸⊷

Her mind was clearing a bit after she got home and found everything was calm. Ellie was still resting as promised, but she'd come down for a light dinner.

"Take your time," Pauline said. "Jack will come get me. Will you be able to take tomorrow off?"

"I'll go in a bit later."

"Okay. I'll be there if she needs anything. How did it happen?"

Jordan knew that her mother's question was more rhetorical than anything, yet she felt guilty for not being able to give a definitive answer.

"We are still trying to figure that out. It's been a weird time."

"I read about clown sightings and murders...It sounds like a nightmare."

"That's pretty much what it has been so far."

They both knew that Pauline couldn't do too much to alleviate the weight she felt on her shoulders. However, she did make their lives easier in so many ways.

"I brought sandwiches earlier if you'd like that for dinner? I can put some fries in the oven before Jack gets here."

"That would be great, thank you."

She went upstairs to the bedroom where Ellie was snuggled up under the covers, looking comfortable.

Get a grip. It could have been worse. She knew, because they'd lived through worse, and survived. Ellie might not be happy to miss work, or about Daniels' suggestions, but she'd enjoy spending time with Meri.

She leaned down to touch her shoulder, waking her gently. "Hey."

Ellie sat up, carefully touching the back of her head.

"Any more pain?"

"Hello to you too...and no. Just a bump. Hanging out here all afternoon actually helped." Reconsidering her words, Ellie said, "I'm sorry I was no help at work."

"Come on. I'm glad you're feeling better."

"I am. And thank you for letting me know about Lisa."

"Yeah. She's safe for now, but she's not talking."

"She needs to understand it's the best she can do for herself, and for Todd." Something sprang to Jordan's mind. She filed it away for later. Perhaps they still had a shot with him. He seemed to genuinely care about Lisa.

"Did you find anything to connect this to the Ronald Jenkins case?"

"Not yet." It wasn't a secret that Ellie was likely to miss some developments in her case. Better to get this over with. "Daniels wants to reassign you and Doss."

To Jordan's surprise, Ellie didn't seem to be concerned about the news.

"I pretty much expected that. There will be other cases. She needs to do the right thing, right out of the gate."

Jordan didn't have time for much of a response. The doorbell rang, announcing Jack's arrival.

"How about we invite them to stay for dinner?" she said. "Only if you're up to it."

"Oh yes. I need to stay awake for a bit, otherwise I won't sleep tonight."

Jordan leaned in to embrace her. She pulled back and softly kissed her forehead. Lucky for her, Ellie didn't always need her to spell out her emotions.

"I love you too," she whispered.

Chapter Twelve

T he next day started out a bit more complicated than either of them would have wished for. Jordan had planned to wait for Kate, who had offered to lend Ellie a hand if needed.

Derek called at 7:56 a.m.

"Where are you?"

"Well—if you recall, yesterday, I took my wife home with a concussion. That's where we are."

"Yeah." He sighed. "Briefing's coming up. You should be here for this."

"I talked to Daniels. I know she's going to reassign...Damn, that's not all, is it?"

"Lisa Garner was about to walk out of the hospital last night. When the doctors tried to convince her to stay, she freaked and started to throw things at them."

"Wow. Any news on that tox screen?"

"Same as Williams, as far as we know. Did Ellie remember anything else?"

"No. Listen, could Kate come over earlier? I don't like leaving Ellie and Meri alone right now."

"Didn't she leave you a message?" Derek asked, surprised. "Her sister asked her to come over today. I can't imagine she didn't tell you. I'm sorry I can't help you, but I need to go. Ask Jack and Pauline?"

"Brilliant idea," she said out loud after he had ended the call. Jack and Pauline were out of town as well to pick up supplies for the bar.

She went back into the kitchen, where Ellie, still in PJs, sat with Meri in her lap.

"Okay, apparently Kate can't come, and I'm supposed to be at the meeting."

"Oh." Ellie barely looked up. "Since I'll be home all day, that works out?"

"You're home sick," Jordan corrected her. "And you're supposed to rest. Didn't you get Kate's message?"

It was a bit of a miracle, and testimony to the excellent support of their family and friends that they hadn't been in a bind like this before. Jordan suppressed a sigh. Ellie had all the right and time to stay home after her injury. Jordan, on the other hand, felt like she had already taken an extraordinary amount of time in the past two years.

"I don't know. I guess it got lost, with everything, I'm sorry." She had Ellie's attention now. "But you need to go." When Jordan was about to protest, Ellie added, "You know there's another option. I'm sure she'd be happy to help."

That silenced her for a few seconds. As usual, Ellie was able to read into that silence.

"I understand you're not one hundred percent comfortable. Remember I'll be here the whole time. I'll be fine, but in the worst-case scenario, Kathryn knows to call 911."

Jordan cast a rueful look at the clock on the wall, time ticking away.

"Okay. I'll call her. I'm sorry, we'll prepare better. It looks like Lisa Garner had some sort of crisis last night."

Ellie didn't comment on that, but Jordan was sure she was thinking of their earlier conversation regarding Daniels' plans.

When she called the number, Kathryn answered after the first ring.

"Jordan, hi. Will you have time to come for dinner?"

"I'm sorry, I can't say yet. Listen...I know this is extremely short notice, but I was wondering if you could come and stay with Ellie and Meri for a few hours today."

"Yes, of course. Is everything okay?"

She probably couldn't blame her for the double check or the surprised tone.

"Ellie has a concussion, but she's going to be okay. I'll just feel better if she isn't all alone with Meri."

"I understand. I'll be there in fifteen minutes at the most."

"Thank you so much. We really appreciate it."

Despite her best efforts, Jordan was late to the briefing. Both Carroll and Daniels were already there. She suppressed a wince and tried to make as few sounds as possible as she sat down in an empty chair next to Detective Wu.

"As we said," Lieutenant Carroll emphasized, "this is an all-hands-on-deck effort. Our priority right now is to get those clowns off the street." He shook his head. "You hear how this sounds? That makes it all the more important."

"Keep one another in the loop," Lieutenant Daniels added. She seemed in a hurry but still took the time to take Jordan aside on the way out.

Pre-empting any criticism, Jordan started talking. "I'm really sorry about being late. I had to set up things at home—"

"I imagined," Daniels dismissed her concerns. "How is Detective Harding doing?"

"She'll be fine. She's resting. I hope. At least that's what I told her to do."

Jordan winced, but to her relief, the lieutenant saw the humor in her statement.

"That's good," she said softly. "Take a moment. Henderson will bring you up to speed."

"Thank you."

"You're welcome. I'm afraid I have to run."

So far so good.

"So, what did I miss?" she asked Derek when she caught up with him. "Garner?"

"It's a mess. They had to sedate her. Last update, she's pretty out of it."

"I have an idea. Let's go."

"Go where?" He sounded skeptical.

"Just a quick errand. If this pans out, things will move."

He cast a look at where Doss, Wu and Murphy were still standing with their supervisors. "It's never boring with you. All right."

Ellie had come to accept some things regarding Jordan and Kathryn's relationship. It wouldn't ever be what Jordan had with Pauline, or how Ellie had felt about her own mother. What they had achieved, though, was remarkable given their history. Ellie had chosen to focus on that. A bit of residual awkwardness was a small price to pay.

"I'm sorry you got hurt," Kathryn said after they sat down with another coffee.

"Thank you. It's not so bad. Well, except for the timing. We have a big case...but to be honest, I'm happy to be spending time with Meri."

"She's beautiful." Kathryn seemed lost in thought for a long moment. "But let me know if you need anything. I could make you lunch…"

"We still have some prepared meals that Jack and Pauline brought us, from the bar."

"Oh. Of course."

"Kathryn, we're really grateful that you're here. I would have been okay on my own, but Jordan worries."

"Yeah. And I'm glad to help, though I know I'm not the first choice. I swear I'm not saying that because I feel sorry for myself, that's just what it is."

Ellie didn't argue. They both knew there was a reason for this.

"Meri is lucky to have many good people in her life, who care about her," she said.

Kathryn was about to say something, when Ellie's cell phone rang.

"Can I get it for you?"

"Oh no, I got it. Thanks."

To her surprise, it was Judy Lawrence on the other end.

"Judy, hi."

"I'm sorry, but you said to call you if there was anything…I didn't call 911 first, because I'm not sure what happened, but I'm worried. Shawn didn't come home last night."

Ellie realized she hadn't been aware that the two of them were living together. "I assume that's unusual? Could he have stayed with anyone?"

"No, he would tell me. His phone is turned off too."

"Look, Judy, I'm at home, but it would be best if you could go to the station, file a report. Ask for Detective Rogers and give him my name. Judy?"

The other woman drew a shaky breath.

"Thank you so much. I guess I was hoping you'd tell me there's nothing to worry about."

Given Judy's proximity to a prior case, and a current one, both related to violent deaths, Ellie wasn't going to take any chances.

"We want to make sure, right? I'll make a call, and someone in Missing Persons will talk to you. We'll figure this out."

When she put her phone back down on the table, Kathryn said, "So this is what sick leave looks like for you."

"I was told to stay away from physical exertion. But this is worrisome. Excuse me for a moment?"

"Sure."

"Harding," Detective Rogers said after picking up the phone. "Aren't you home with a concussion?"

Ellie suppressed a sigh. "Yes. You might want to check in with Jordan and Derek on this one. Judy Lawrence..."

"Wait a moment. That Judy Lawrence?"

"Yes. She knew the victim in my latest case, and she thinks her boyfriend is missing. I met him briefly...I'm not sure what to think. I told her to go to the station to file a report."

"And this is related to the clown murders?" he asked.

"There was a clown mask left behind in the victim's house, so yes, that's what we assume."

"All right, I'll check with Carpenter and Henderson," he said. "Get well soon."

"Thanks."

"Poor Ms. Lawrence. Her name keeps coming up."

"Yeah. Thank you." *Keep me in the loop*, Ellie almost said, but for the moment, everyone had more important things to do.

❦

Todd Williams rolled his eyes, not subtle about his reaction when he saw who his visitors were.

"Don't tell me you still have no idea who killed Randy. I can't help you. It's your job to find out."

They went inside, and Jordan closed the door, leaning against it.

"I don't know, Todd. The more I think about it, the more it seems to me that you could help us a little more."

"What's that supposed to mean?" he scoffed.

"I understand that you're afraid. Lisa is too. But the people who did this aren't going to stop as long as you stay silent."

"I don't like what you're implying. I lost my best friend. They took my girlfriend, did God knows what to her."

"Why?"

He shook his head as if confused.

"Why would anyone do this to you? Because you made deals with the wrong people? Or Randy messed up on the job? He got into trouble with a customer not so long ago."

"I told you, the guy who sells me the pot is mellow. I'm sure you checked him out already. The cocaine he got us, that was a one-time thing, and I always paid on time."

"You're right, we checked him out, and he confirms your story." An easy arrest, though it hadn't helped them with the clowns. Jordan didn't think he played any role in this. There was another avenue she wanted to follow.

"So, what's the problem?"

"Why aren't you with Lisa right now?" Jordan asked. "After everything she's been through?"

"What? I wouldn't be able to see her anyway. They gave her something to sleep."

"Okay," she said, "let me phrase this another way. She seems to have taken good care of you since your own abduction, yet you're angry at her."

"Because she cheated on me!" he snapped. "Okay? There you have it. Yes, she made me soup and all, but that doesn't make it go away. Guy's bragging in my face, so when he comes to the garage, I tell Randy to get back at him."

Derek cast her a quick, impressed glance. Jordan kept her expression neutral, though she was thrilled her hunch was playing out the way she'd expected it.

"You asked him to mess with the guy's car."

"Not too badly, not to hurt or kill him, for Pete's sake! Just a little inconvenience, nothing you'd respond to by cutting off someone's hand." He shuddered, then elaborated, "This guy's car needed a special kind of oil. When he came in for his tune-up, Randy used the wrong kind on purpose. I don't know all the details, but it damaged the engine. He figured it out and threatened to sue Randy, but then he didn't, for some reason."

Because he had bigger plans for revenge? How did a story of betrayal and property damage turn into an elaborate case of abduction and murder?

"You're not going to charge me for any of that, right?" Todd asked, alarmed all of a sudden. "There was not a scratch on the guy."

"If he had anything to do with the murder, taking you to court is not going to be his priority," Derek surmised. "What else can you tell us about him?"

"You'd have to ask Lisa, she slept with him," Williams grumbled. "Tall, blond, looks like a surfer dude. She says he came to the bar."

"His name," Jordan reminded him to get back on track.

"Carl something."

She wasn't sure whether to be disappointed or relieved.

"Okay. I'm sure we'll get those records from Mr. Quentin now. Thank you, Todd."

"Yeah, I know. You'll be in touch."

"Wow," Derek said. "How did you figure that out?"

"I'm not sure you want to know."

"Don't worry. I know everything about your troubled past already."

"Funny. But honestly, what else could it be? He was hanging out with his buddy drinking and getting high while she worked night shifts. For him to be this mad at her, after everything, that's the only thing I could think of. And you're one to talk about a troubled past."

He laughed, acknowledging that there was some truth to her statement.

"Before we get into that, let's get a hold of Esposito? By which I mean, you do it. She still has a soft spot for you."

Jordan was already on the phone. Some things weren't worth arguing over.

"Okay, Val, this is the situation," she said, explaining their progress after she had put the A.D.A. on speaker. "Let me know how soon you can get me that warrant."

"Wow. There I thought you'd buy me dinner first."

Derek snickered. She ignored him.

"I'll call you," Valerie said, realizing quickly that Jordan wasn't in the mood.

Chapter Thirteen

With the new developments, and no update from anyone, Ellie didn't especially feel like a nap. After a morning of playing with Meri and helping Kathryn load the dishwasher, she had to reluctantly admit she could use some rest.

Her mind kept going back to that moment in the woods. Lisa's unexpected reaction, and the question of how Judy Lawrence's story was related.

Something Rogers had said stuck with her...about Lawrence being the target of a ritualistic crime more than once. She had escaped a serial killer, then his fan club. The main instigators in the group were still serving prison sentences for trying to re-enact his crimes. Ellie didn't think they cared about the coins, even though they had paid attention to detail when it came to their hero's M.O. Judy's coins had been the trophy.

Now, Jenkins, a fellow coin collector, had been murdered by someone who left a clown mask behind.

What was the connection between those cases spanning over years?

So much for rest.

While they were updating their colleagues on their progress, Valerie called to notify Jordan that they'd be able to request Quentin's records. Derek's phone rang while she was still on hers.

"The hospital," he mouthed.

"Thank you. I owe you," Jordan said to Valerie, making her laugh.

"I appreciate that you acknowledge it. Good luck."

"Okay, where are we at with Lisa?" she asked. "No bad news I hope?"

"No. She's awake and ready to talk."

"That's great. Let's split up? Wu, you want to come serve the warrant with me?"

He nodded. "Sure."

"All right. Let's go."

As everyone got to their feet, there was a knock on the door, and Detective Rogers from Missing Persons walked in.

"Hey, I'm sorry to disturb, but I wanted to tell you I have Ms. Judy Lawrence with me."

"What happened?" Jordan asked, aware that she sounded anxious.

"She reported her boyfriend missing. It sounds like we have a case."

Technically, that was still Maria's case.

"Damn. She seemed to be doing well. That has to be a blow."

Derek had caught Jordan's hesitation. "If you'd like to talk to her, I'm sure Detective Wu will take care of the warrant."

"Either you'll join me later, or I'll get those records back to you ASAP," Wu promised.

The truth was, Jordan wasn't even sure whether she wanted to talk to Judy Lawrence, but she felt she owed her. Too many things kept coming back to her, and it couldn't be a coincidence.

She deserved peace.

"Sounds good to me," she agreed and then went to follow Rogers.

She was impressed at how Judy was holding up, compared to when she had last seen her.

"Hey."

"Hey," Judy said softly. "So, we meet again."

"Detective Rogers told me about Shawn. I'm sorry."

"Thank you. This is not like him. And I'm starting to wonder, with everything...if I'm bad luck."

"You're not. Don't ever think that."

There was, however, something about the victim of a crime that attracted the worst of people. Their shared history had put them both on the radar of a disturbing fan group. Part of Shriver's interest in Jordan was clearly related to that same story.

"I don't know what to think anymore," Judy said with a sigh. "I told the detective...Ellie, that he said some cryptic things the other night, about people who get away with all kinds of bad stuff. I wasn't sure what he was talking about."

"Earlier, Ms. Lawrence spoke to Detective Harding who told her to come here," Rogers clarified. "It's a good thing she did."

"You think this has to do with Ronald's death?" Judy asked anxiously.

"We don't want to jump to conclusions, but I'd like it if you could stay with a friend, or have someone over tonight?"

Judy nodded, her expression resigned. "I'll call my sister."

"You do that. We'll notify you if there's anything new," Rogers said.

After Judy had called her sister Meg, she and Jordan shook hands before Rogers saw Judy out.

Jordan leaned against the wall, feeling lightheaded all of a sudden—and glad she'd escaped the conversation this might have turned into.

She, too, left the room, intent on checking if it was too late to join Wu.

Unfortunately, the warrant would only cover the client list and security footage of the day, not the duffel bags she'd seen in Quentin's office the other day.

⚯

"Do you know when Jordan will be back tonight?" Kathryn asked. Since today the weather was unusually mild for the time of year, Ellie had decided she wanted to take Meri out in her stroller. She couldn't sleep all day or even try. And the doctor had told her to take it easy, not to stop moving altogether.

Kathryn's question surprised her.

"I'm not sure. Do you need to head home?"

"Oh no, I have time. I was just wondering if you wanted to visit us sometime. We made changes in the apartment."

Kathryn and her husband Jim had moved from their trailer home into an apartment the previous year. Time passed by quickly.

"Maybe not tonight, but sometime soon, for sure." Ellie snuck a glance at her cell phone, but there was no message or missed call. "I don't know about you, but I could use some more caffeine. How about here?" she pointed at the café across the street from them. "Jordan used to come here often after Meri was born and I was at work."

"Sure, why not?"

Kathryn looked thoughtful, making Ellie wonder if she'd missed something.

After they'd found a seat and ordered, she said, "I know there's rarely a lot of time, but I swear we'll come by soon."

"Thank you." Kathryn gave her a small smile. "Ellie, can I ask you a question?"

"Of course." A moment later, she asked herself if she was going to regret her quick answer.

"Okay. I'm sure you have come across this. If someone is in for murder, under what circumstances would they be released early? Surely staying under the radar on the inside wouldn't be enough?"

Ellie could feel her jaw drop. At the same time, Meri dropped her plush toy, a colorful fish, and started crying. Priorities.

"That depends," she said after rescuing Fish and consoling her daughter. "I would hope it started out with a strong case. If there were any doubts as to intent, and of course, guilt..."

Kathryn gave a bitter laugh. "I have trouble imagining that."

Ellie felt a chill creep up her back. Kathryn couldn't mean what Ellie was thinking. No way.

"I can tell from your expression that you have an idea who I'm talking about."

"Well, then, no, I can't imagine that a bit of good behavior would be enough. That case was clear. A cop died."

"You promise me that there's no way TJ will get out?"

Somehow it was worse to hear her say it. Worse, even, there was no way either one of them could keep this from Jordan.

"You know that's not for me to decide, but I can't imagine a scenario where he'd get away with what he's done. Why do you think that?"

Even Meri looked anxious, and Ellie lifted her onto her lap.

Kathryn shrugged. "He called me. Was all polite and friendly, and asked if I would speak in his favor. I told him there was no way."

She had taken the call though.

"To whom?"

"The parole board? I don't know. I told Jim, and he said to ask Jordan."

Ellie sat back, unsure what to answer.

"When did this happen?"

"A few days ago. I tried to talk to Jordan on the phone, but you're always so busy. I was hoping that maybe tonight, we could sit down and talk about this..."

"Kathryn. No. I mean, I want to talk to her first, and I promise you we'll look into this as soon as possible. It makes no sense anyway that he could be up for parole so soon. Besides, you don't owe him anything."

"I guess I could argue with that," Kathryn said wryly. "But I don't want him anywhere near me, or my family. I don't know, maybe he was just messing with me, as usual."

"Why did you take his call?"

"Good question. I guess I was curious to find out what he wanted? Never in a million years did I expect anything like this."

"I wouldn't worry too much. No matter who says anything in his favor, there are many others who can testify to the fact that he's a cold-blooded killer."

"I hope you're right," Kathryn said.

Ellie hugged her daughter a little tighter, spooked by the fact that there was a biological connection between her baby and TJ Pratt.

Unimaginable.

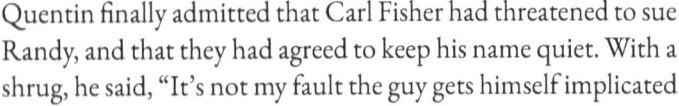

Quentin finally admitted that Carl Fisher had threatened to sue Randy, and that they had agreed to keep his name quiet. With a shrug, he said, "It's not my fault the guy gets himself implicated in a murder case. I didn't even know this was about the girl. Jesus, Randy. I had no idea that's what happened."

Jordan exchanged a look with Wu. Even though the other detective met the owner for the first time, she could sense that he, too, had doubts.

"About that video footage..."

Quentin gave an exaggerated sigh. "Come on. Sara will show you."

In short, Jordan hadn't missed much.

Behind the reception counter, Sara was as unfazed as ever. "I'll make you a copy," she said. "But here's the day you wanted, if you'd like to take a look."

"Yes, please."

Wu and Murphy hadn't been on the case until today, and this part had previously belonged to Ellie and Maria, so he didn't notice right away. Jordan did, her hand going to her phone.

"Yeah, that's him," Quentin made a positive ID. He sighed. "I was hoping that we could all just forget about this stupid thing."

"Hm."

"That's all you have to say? Is he your killer?"

"We shouldn't make any assumptions," Jordan said. "For now, he's a person of interest. Thank you, Mr. Quentin."

Outside the business, Wu asked, "This was pretty quick. You know the guy?"

"Unfortunately," she mumbled. "I'll tell you in the car."

❦

They were on their way to meet with the lieutenant, one of them anyway, in the briefing room so everyone would be updated on the new developments. A few minutes early, Jordan took the moment to sneak away to the break room for some coffee. While she was proud of Ellie for her instincts, she didn't look forward to telling Judy that her boyfriend might be implicated in a murder, maybe two.

She drank from her coffee, contemplating the food choices when Derek walked in. It might be a tad petty, Jordan reflected, but she was struggling with the recent changes too. She was well aware that Carroll and Daniels did the best they could with the political framework they'd been given, but she was tired. Building a rapport with new colleagues who came with a different approach, it was part of the job, but the timing wasn't great.

"You're all right?" Derek asked.

She shrugged. "We don't know for sure that he killed two men. But for Judy, this is bad either way."

"Have you heard from Ellie?"

"Kathryn's staying with her and Meri. I was going to call her too."

"I can go by Carl Fisher's apartment if you'd prefer to head home..."

"No. I'll call Judy, and after the meeting we can go."

"What are you going to tell her?"

She sighed. "If you have any great ideas, hit me now."

Derek's gaze was sympathetic.

Chapter Fourteen

"We're good," Ellie assured her.

"Where are you?" Jordan hadn't expected the voices in the background.

"We took a walk and stopped for a coffee. It's allowed, right?"

"Of course." There was something in Ellie's tone that gave her pause. "You're really okay?"

"Yes, of course. It's a little loud in here. We'll continue this tonight?"

"I won't be too late," Jordan promised. She would have liked to talk to Ellie longer, but she had to trust her—and she still had that other call to make.

There was hardly any way to sugarcoat the developments regarding Carl Fisher a.k.a. Shawn. Jordan tried to break the news to Judy as diplomatically as possible, but it seemed the woman had a sixth sense about the dire implications. Perhaps it was better that way. Safer for Judy.

"If he contacts you in any way, I'd like you to call us immediately."

"You think he's in some kind of trouble. Something he did?"

"We don't know, Judy," she said softly. "We just want to be on the safe side."

The other woman laughed bitterly. "That always works out so well, doesn't it? I'm sorry. I swear I'm going to keep it together. Nothing is that bad in the grand scheme of things, right?"

"Like I said, your safety is priority. We'll keep in touch."

"Sure. I can stay with Meg for a bit."

"Good." Jordan watched her colleagues file into the briefing room. "I'll have to let you go. We'll talk soon."

"I'm afraid we will." This time, there was a bit of real humor to her words.

For the second time today, she walked into a meeting that had already started. Jordan hoped this wouldn't become a habit.

"We know this about Carl Fisher," Wu explained. "He threatened to sue Randy Fowler, then settled with his boss. He's also dating Judy Lawrence under an alias, and he's missing."

"We were going over to his apartment right after this," Derek announced, and Jordan nodded.

"Under the circumstances we were able to cut through the red tape quickly. We'll update the nightshift...unless we get lucky."

"We could use a little luck," Carroll muttered. "Let's see if I got this straight. This guy has a family, he got on Williams' radar for sleeping with his girlfriend, and he dated Ms. Lawrence using a different name. What kind of bizarre soap opera is this?"

Jordan thought he had a point, even though everything regarding these cases was bizarre.

"The kind that he'll have the time watching when he's retired," Derek joked, not quietly enough.

"I'm glad you're having fun, Henderson. Now get out of here. You all know what to do." Before they left for Fisher's apartment, he held her back.

"How's Harding doing?"

"Good," Jordan said. "I think she'll be okay to come back to work after the weekend."

"I'm glad to hear that. Tell her I'd be offended if she missed my retirement party."

"Yes, sir. I think she knows, but I'll pass it on."

"Now find me that guy," he said grimly. "We've had enough of those criminal pranksters."

"There must be a connection to the garage," Jordan said when they were in the car.

"We looked at the employees," Derek reminded her. "Nothing stood out, DUI for one of them when he was eighteen, almost ten years ago."

"That doesn't have to mean anything. We still don't know what was in those duffel bags."

"Maybe...gym clothes?"

"Come on."

"Just trying to lighten the mood here."

Twenty minutes later, the building manager opened the door of Fisher's apartment to them. The man's jaw dropped, and Jordan and Derek nearly had the same reaction at the empty place.

No furniture, no clothes, nothing on the walls.

"I want to say, this guy's been ghosting us," Derek mumbled.

Jordan wasn't sure whether she wanted to laugh or punch the bare wall.

Ellie had spent most of the rest of the day trying to figure out how to best raise the subject. As she expected, Jordan looked tired when she finally made it home. They said goodbye to

Kathryn, and Ellie went to get Meri ready for the night while Jordan headed for a hot shower.

When Jordan returned to the kitchen, Ellie took a cold beer out of the fridge.

"I'm still following doctor's orders, but I thought you might want one."

Jordan surveyed the table Ellie had set. Perhaps a candlelight dinner in the middle of the week was a little too obvious.

"You were right about Shawn," Jordan said. "His real name is Carl Fisher. He also had an affair with Lisa Garner."

"Okay...What's next?"

"He's gone. His apartment was practically stripped down." Jordan took a sip of her beer. "Now you. How did it go with Kathryn? I have the feeling I won't like it, so let's get it over with."

"I can't keep anything from you, can I? Not that I'm trying. And this time, it's not her fault."

Ellie sat across from her. "This might be nothing, but I think it's better if we have a game plan here. She got a call from TJ Pratt. He asked her to testify on his behalf."

"That's bullshit." Jordan didn't mince words. "It's over and done."

"I asked around a bit, and I was able to get some information. Apparently, TJ's plan is to convince the parole board that he found religion, and he wants to do good—outside of prison, of course."

"Wow. All right." Jordan shook her head. "This is different. Brazen, but no one's going to fall for this."

Her quick dismissal of the issue was exactly what Ellie needed.

"Right? I didn't want to bother you with this at work. I don't think there's anything to worry about."

"No. Not at all."

"Should we tell Kate about this? Just as a warning. He might try to get some press."

"Let him." Jordan took another sip, no doubt imagining the backlash Pratt would unleash if he tried to go through with the plan. No one would buy his act. The wounds his actions had caused were still too fresh. Kate remembered. So did Jensen Baker's family. They all did.

"I'm really sorry."

"It's okay. You're right though, we should warn Kate. And perhaps give Jill a heads-up. She'll bring the right angle."

"Good idea. I'll text her. Perhaps we could all have dinner tomorrow, Kate and Derek too."

Jordan laughed. "This is what you call taking it easy?"

"I can't nap all day."

"You sure got things done. I like that in a woman."

"Lucky me..."

Jordan's smile presented a welcome distraction from the dire possibilities. Escapism might be a part of it, but Ellie was glad about the way she dealt with the recent news. Perhaps they'd never even get to what could be the most frightening part.

There was no way in hell Pratt's scheme could succeed.

No, no, no. Predictably, Jordan lay awake as the minutes crept by at a pace that seemed mocking to her.

She had always been good at coming up with worst-case scenarios. She still was, even though life with Ellie put her mind at ease in a way she'd never imagined. Now this. Jordan had done her best to remove TJ Pratt, the man who had slept with Kathryn once, from her mind. It had been consensual according to Kathryn, but not without consequences.

Jordan considered Jack Carpenter her father. Jim, Kathryn's husband, had been in her life for a while. He'd done nothing much to make it better, but he was a far cry from Pratt, the career criminal. There was no realistic chance that he'd make it out given his well documented crimes. She hated that she even had to think about this for one moment.

That he could find out about Meri.

Before that happened, they'd rally their allies around them. Fortunately, some of them were as angry as Jordan was.

Saturday morning, Kathryn came over once more while Jordan spent a couple of hours at the station. Later, she and Ellie prepared the table for dinner. When Derek called, she put him on speaker and set the phone on the counter.

"We're still coming," he said. "I ran into Maria earlier, and I promised her to ask you if you have a couple more seats at the table."

Ellie studied Jordan closely. For what they were about to discuss, it might not be the worst idea to have another cop and an A.D.A., both good friends, at the table, but she wanted Jordan to make the choice.

"Sure, I'm good with that if they are. We're just ordering in, remember?"

"No problem. Should we bring anything?"

Ellie could tell by his question that Jordan hadn't raised the subject yet. Now that there were going to be more people, she wondered if she should ask Kate to come over earlier, then reconsidered. This was painful enough, and everyone that would be in the room had an interest in keeping Pratt behind bars.

"Not this time. We're still waiting for that day when you and Kate invite us on the boat."

"This spring. I swear."

"Okay. Maybe bring wine. See you later," she said before ending the call. "Kathryn seemed okay this morning, right? So perhaps we don't need to freak out either. I bet you he hasn't even tried to start the process, because he knows everyone will laugh in his face."

Ellie agreed, though she was relieved they'd be able to take some pre-emptive measures. In no scenario would either one of them let this man anywhere near their daughter.

Chapter Fifteen

"**Y**ou've got to be kidding me. This man ever gets out, I'll shoot the son of a bitch myself. Sorry, Jordan."

"I think Jordan understands. We all understand," Derek said after a moment of tense silence, reaching out to take Kate's hand. "I'd still like to start over and pretend none of us heard what you just said."

She glared at him. "What, you think their house is bugged? Come on. You know what he did."

"Yes, and he should stay behind bars because of it. This is not realistic, right?"

"Some people can turn their lives around. Pratt—he's not one of them," Jordan said, relieved she'd listened to Ellie. When Kate and Derek were the first to show up, they had filled them in right away. "But Derek is right. We wanted to give you a heads-up, and pool resources."

"Is he going to contact me? I'll tell him where he can stick his story." A hint of fear was piercing Kate's anger.

"I don't think that's up to him," Ellie said. "But someone might want to speak to you on his behalf, if they're going forward. We're going to stop it in its tracks. Any lawyer will soon realize that an appeal is not realistic. And Jill already said that her editor might be interested in telling the story from a reasonable angle."

They finally sat down in the living room.

"This might actually be helpful," Derek remarked. "It will remind the people that we put a lot of heavyweights away."

"Or it might make him look sympathetic," Kate said morosely. "All right, can we get to the wine? I don't want to deal with this sober."

"I can't blame you," Jordan told her. "I'll be right back."

⁕

Of their friends present, Valerie Esposito was the only one who hadn't worked and lived in the city when Pratt teamed up with a crime lord from out of town. Their alliance had brought terror on various people, including Kate who lost her fiancé in an ambush.

"I'll be glad to reach out to my predecessor," Valerie said. "He might even want to make a statement. I can see how this is unsettling for everyone, but you can all relax. This is not going to happen."

"Can I quote you on that?" Jill asked.

"Normally I'd be careful with that, but in this case...We're safe."

"Great. Crisis averted," Jordan said. "I just wanted to make sure we're aware...and we'll keep each other in the loop."

"I understand. It's off the record until you tell me otherwise. Thanks for having me here."

She nodded to Jill. "No problem. As you can see, we're not entirely unselfish here."

After all these years it was a relief that her friends, old and new, were on the same page. No one had any doubts or questions when it came to her relationship with Pratt—it was simple, for her, for them.

She had tortured herself over the idea of biological destiny, but that was before Meri. The reality of her own child had confirmed that choices counted more than anything. She and Ellie would make the good ones for Meri.

She cast a look over at Kate, wishing she could do more for her. She had coped with her fiancé's death, found love again, but a bad surprise like this brought back the raw anger.

"Okay, I think the food should be here soon."

As if on cue, the doorbell rang, perfect timing. Everyone around the table could use some comfort.

※

"We have a hit," Jordan said, not even trying to keep the triumph out of her voice. The message she'd gotten from Anna Crawford, head of the lab, might not get her a warrant for the garage, but it was one step closer. "There were some prints on the clown mask," she explained to the other attendees of Monday's briefing. "They belong to Dylan Hastings, one of Randy's co-workers at the garage. Let's bring him in and ask him how his prints ended up on evidence in a murder case."

"You and Henderson go," Carroll said. "Harding, I'd like to see you in my office."

Ellie didn't look concerned, and given what he had told her the other day, Jordan assumed it would simply be a follow-up after her sick leave.

Derek was driving, so she leaned back in her seat, trying to anticipate what they might find at the garage.

"You heard anything else about Pratt?" he asked.

"No. Thank God. I imagine after Jill's story, that will be it."

"Yeah." To her relief, he didn't try to deepen the subject. "So, what do we know about this Hastings guy, other than the DUI from a decade ago?"

"He went on to become a mechanic, paid all his bills on time. Not even a parking ticket. He's been working for Quentin for five years."

"Fowler didn't have the job that long," Derek remembered. "He only came on board a year ago."

"Let's see what Hastings has to tell us."

Sara at the reception greeted them with a polite smile.

"Detectives. Mr. Quentin isn't in today. May I help you with something?"

"You may," Jordan said. "Where can we find Mr. Hastings?"

"Oh, funny you should ask."

"Why is that?"

"He didn't come to work today. He hasn't called yet either."

"Thank you."

They stepped aside, and Derek asked, "We'll talk to the other guys?"

"Not yet. I'd like to check if Dylan's at home, and I don't want them to tip him off."

"You don't think Sara will?"

"She might. That's why we have to go now."

❦

On the way, they had called for a unit to back them up. Officers Marshall and Martin were already parked in front of the building when they arrived.

Hastings was definitely home, sounds coming from inside his apartment. He didn't react to the doorbell, knocking or the request to open the door.

"It's going to be one of those days," Jordan muttered.

"Looks like it."

"Mr. Hastings, this is—"

She was interrupted by a piercing scream and quickly stepped aside.

"Your turn to kick the door." Not that they were keeping count, but Derek didn't argue otherwise.

A moment later, they were standing in front of Dylan Hastings, who jumped up from the couch. He was in his underwear.

"What the fuck? Did someone swat me?"

They could barely hear him over the screams still emanating from the TV. After a quick glance, Jordan spun around, feeling sick to her stomach. Not your traditional horror—or adult—film.

"Would you mind?"

He finally paused the movie, the image frozen on a rather grotesque scene.

"Did the guys from the garage send you?"

"We need to ask you some questions," Derek said. "You better put on some clothes."

"What if I say no?"

"Your prints were found on evidence, in the house of a murder victim. If you have nothing to do with it, you might want to clear it up?"

"I can't believe this," he sulked. "You're going to watch me dress? You want to come to my bedroom?"

Jordan didn't deign to answer.

"No thanks," Derek said, but he went to check the window and fire escape after Hastings had disappeared into his bedroom. He emerged a few minutes later dressed in cargo pants and a T-shirt.

Derek waited until Hastings had left with the uniforms. "That garage is one place I'd never go for maintenance," he said. "The people working there are insane."

Jordan cast another look at the picture on the screen, wholeheartedly agreeing with him.

She sat across from him in the interrogation room. Hastings didn't yet seem to appreciate how much trouble he was in. Not very original—he was hoping the scene from the movie had rattled her. Jordan had seen these tactics before. Hell, she had experienced some true horror herself.

"Mr. Hastings," she said as she tossed the mask enclosed in an evidence bag onto the table. "This is yours?"

Derek sat next to her, but Hastings remained focused on Jordan.

"You really don't like my tastes, do you? Too bad. As for this, I'm not sure."

"You're not sure? Why is that?"

"Might have worn it for Halloween or something, but if it's that particular one, I don't know."

"So, you own more than one?" Derek asked.

"I didn't say that. I wore a similar one for Halloween."

"Which Halloween?"

Hastings all but rolled his eyes at Derek. "Couple of years ago. I'd have to go through my pictures."

"We'd appreciate that. All right. Do you know a Ronald Jenkins?"

He shook his head. "Never heard of him."

"You know anything about valuable coins?"

Hastings started laughing. "You're really fishing, aren't you? I'm not sure what you're getting at, but sure, perhaps I wore that mask, and someone took it from the basement. Whatever they did with it, it's not my problem."

"You might be wrong about that." Jordan took a sip of her coffee, waited a few more heartbeats. "We have a warrant for your apartment."

"So? You might not like my choice of movies, but they're not illegal."

"I'm not talking about a horror flick," she clarified. "We already have the mask with your prints on it. The way it's going, I'm sure we could justify asking you for DNA. You worked with Randy Fowler, another murder victim. Don't you think all of this is happening awfully close to home?"

"You tell me, Detective." He grinned. "You think you can charge me with something?"

"Carl Fisher came to the garage. He was aware of Jenkins and his coin collection. He also got into trouble with Randy. Did he ask you to take care of it?"

"Me? Come on. I didn't even see the guy when all that trouble with Randy started."

"Funny. We have you on video talking to him, reassuring him."

He did a bit of a double take but quickly composed himself. "Mr. Quentin needed someone on it. Fisher was going to sue."

"On it, what exactly does that mean?"

"Offering a discount, something like that."

"Hm. All right."

"Does that mean I can go?"

"No, that's not what it means."

"Then I want to talk to a lawyer—"

Everyone in the room turned to the door when after a quick rap, Officer Libby Marshall came inside.

"Jordan, can I speak to you?"

Realizing that Libby was well aware that this was an inconvenient moment, Jordan assumed her request had to be urgent.

She got up to join her at the door where Libby informed her, "There's been another sighting. Weston Elementary."

"Don't tell me it's a clown sighting." Dylan Hastings couldn't have heard what she'd said. Nevertheless, he laughed, a cackling sound almost as alarming as his choice in movies.

Chapter Sixteen

"I'm starting to think this town is haunted for real. Were all these decorations this morbid last year? I don't think I noticed." Jordan shared her observations with Derek as they were walking from the parking lot to the entrance of Weston Elementary School where uniformed officers had already taped off the area. In the distance, one of them was talking to a group of parents.

"You had other things on your mind," Derek acknowledged.

"Yeah. I sure did. I'm changing my mind now. No trick-or-treating for Meri. She's going to have nightmares for years."

"It might be a little early for that," he agreed.

Given recent events, the sight of a clown sneaking around the premises had triggered a lockdown.

When they were about to greet the officer at the door, Sam Potts came running towards them.

"Guess what?" she said, sounding excited. "We got him. He's one of the mechanics at Quentin's." Sam pointed to the squad car where a bored-looking Chris Atwood stood leaning against the driver's side door. A man was sitting in the backseat.

"Great job," Jordan returned. "What can you tell us about him?"

"He was peering into windows, scaring the kids. The teacher called 911 and triggered a lockdown. He was still on the school grounds when we found him."

"All right. You take him in. We catch up with you later."

She looked around the place, at the worried parents in the distance, and suppressed a sigh. It wasn't time to celebrate yet, but this was an important step. With the lockdown lifted, they could reunite scared children with their equally scared parents and talk to the teacher.

They found her in the principal's office. Both women seemed shocked, but more angry about the situation as the kindergarten teacher described what had happened.

"He didn't really do anything or try to come in, but with that grisly mask...I couldn't take the risk," she said. "He could have had a gun."

"You did the right thing," Jordan assured her.

"We were lucky," the principal added.

It was hard to argue with that statement. It lingered for a few seconds, reminding all of them how much worse this day could have gotten. Jordan thought they had reason to be carefully optimistic.

Hastings was conferring with a public defender at this moment, and they had apprehended another clown. The web was tightening around those criminal comedians.

❧

"Where's the detective?" Hastings asked when Ellie stepped into the room. "I am ready to talk."

"You can talk to me. I'm Detective Harding. So, did you refresh your memory on how that mask ended up in Mr. Jenkins' house?"

It was one of those moments when everyone had a job to do, and she couldn't just sit on her hands, behind her desk. When Jordan and Derek returned, they would interrogate Hastings' colleague Jimmy Bryan who had been picked up at the school. In a quick phone call, they had determined that Ellie would continue with Hastings. It made sense, as it put more pressure on both men to talk. They'd sort out the rest later.

"One of the other guys must have taken it there. I was never in that house."

"You were on the grounds of the amusement park the night Randy was killed, and Todd Williams was kidnapped?"

He looked uncomfortable, glancing at his lawyer who nodded. "Mr. Hastings has decided to come clean," he said.

"I was there," Hastings confirmed. "I got the call, I went...I had no idea that they were going to shoot somebody, I swear."

"Who are they?"

"I don't know."

"Come on," Ellie said, disbelief coloring her tone. "You know that one of your co-workers was just arrested? Coming clean is a good idea, but you have to make up your mind, and you have to be quick. If he talks first..."

"Yeah, I know you're supposed to say that, but I can't help you, and he won't either. Look, I know he was in it too because I recognized the voice. That's all. Just a coincidence. It's one of the rules. You stick to the plan, you don't try to identify anyone, or you're out."

"Out of what?" She was beginning to get irritated. This was supposed to be a quick wrap-up, given that they had compelling points to make him tell the truth.

"The game. It was supposed to be just a game, okay? You want to get back at someone, you find your teammates and go for it. Stupid Randy almost got the shop shut down because of

Todd and his girlfriend. I never imagined someone would end up dead."

"Or lose a hand?" Ellie prompted, instinctively leaning back a few inches. Hastings turned green-ish so fast she was afraid he might throw up. This was new information though, something that might tie all the cases together. A game. A stupid game in which people lost their lives. It was one of those days that she wanted to give up on humanity altogether...

But they still had a case to solve first.

"Okay, I want you to tell me everything you know. How did you find the game, how you play, everything you were involved in."

"You'll take his cooperation into consideration?" the lawyer asked.

"That's not for me to decide as you know, but you'll definitely be in a better position if you can offer the A.D.A. something of worth. Try to provide as much detail as possible. The amusement park, Mr. Jenkins, Lisa Garner."

He seemed to finally grasp the gravity of his situation.

"I don't know who the other guys are," Jimmy Bryan declared. "Except for Dylan, obviously, but I didn't know until after the first couple of times."

Jordan shared an incredulous look with Detective Wu who stood in the corner, arms crossed over his chest. She turned to the suspect and sat across from him.

"You mention Dylan, your co-worker who's spilling his guts to my colleague as we speak. You know it's a bit of a race right now. We have two murders, kidnappings and a few instances that could have turned equally bad...Whoever gives us names first, wins."

"But I don't have names! He doesn't either. That's not how you play the game. And we weren't going to kill anyone."

"Interesting. A game where you bring guns and tools to dismember people, ropes and duct tape...but killing someone wasn't on your mind."

"I swear! I got an invitation, okay? It was supposed to be fun, pranks. Like appearing out of the woods and saying boo."

Jordan thought of the man who nearly had an accident, or the woman in the parking garage. She suppressed a shudder, frustration, anger, and a memory she couldn't give any room to at the moment.

"You and Dylan both got that invitation, or did you recruit him?"

"He recognized my voice. I didn't know the others. We're not supposed to take the mask off, ever. That's the whole point."

"So, about that invitation."

"Via email. Dylan, he's in a lot of groups online, I don't know. It probably came from one of those."

"You have to be more specific," Wu reminded him.

"I don't know. Horror-based stuff?"

Jordan knew they had to be careful. Otherwise, there were too many people who would chalk up this type of behavior to the consumption of horror movies and video games, rather than the actions of entitled young men.

"Yeah, we know about his collection," she said. Adult movies with violent sexual elements. Under the circumstances, it wouldn't be hard to get a warrant for his electronic devices too. "So, why the kindergarten?"

"It was supposed to be my final challenge," he said. "It's tougher now that the police have been looking for us."

"Why don't we take a break and get back to it in a few minutes?"

"There I thought Shriver's story was wild," Wu commented when they had left the room to get another coffee. "This is a mess."

While she agreed with him, Jordan couldn't help thinking that parts of this mess weren't shocking or new. Even Shriver fit the bill to some point. He, too, had felt entitled, to a promotion, to women's affection. Alicia Fox's. Jordan's.

"Let's get that coffee," she said. "The sooner we can sort this all out, the better."

✦

They ran into Ellie and Valerie in the hallway, stopping for a quick update.

"That's what I like to hear. Things are moving," Valerie commented.

"Yes, finally. It's been overdue," Jordan agreed. "Bad luck for these two that they could identify one another. We find the others, and..."

"Game over," she and Ellie said at the same time. Valerie looked amused, but her next words had everyone sober up quickly.

"All right, keep at it. They might have been stupid and careless, but two people still died. There has to be some accountability."

"I agree," Jordan said. "Don't worry. We'll get there."

She knew Ellie and their new colleagues were just as determined. A win would be a win for all of them, including Daniels, who had been off to a rough start.

✦

Both Hastings and his co-worker seemed to understand that cooperating was their best bet. The next step would be to figure out where the invitations for "the game" had initially come from.

There was something that struck Ellie as a strange coincidence, though she was reluctant to mention it to Jordan in front of all their colleagues, especially Wu and Murphy who were still new around here.

It might matter, though, and she didn't want to be responsible for holding up the investigation, so she took Jordan aside during a five-minute break.

"Okay, let me do this real quick so it's out of the way and you can hopefully tell me I'm imagining things."

"This is already beyond bizarre," Jordan acknowledged. "Go ahead."

"Yes. All right." Ellie took a deep breath, realizing this wasn't easy even if it was just the two of them. If she was tired of going there, it was infinitely worse for Jordan. At least Pratt's attempts were unlikely to go anywhere—that was a blessing. "So, there's a game, people get invitations to play...certain people, like those two co-workers who wanted to get back at Randy for almost shutting down the garage. I don't know, maybe it's far-fetched...but what if Randy or Todd were players too?"

"What makes you think that?"

"The love triangle with Lisa...and Carl Fisher. There's a theme of revenge, punishment..." She hesitated. Jordan waited patiently. "And there's Fisher, aka Shawn, Judy's boyfriend. She said he wasn't jealous of her relationship with Jenkins, but do we really know that for sure? Fisher could have been a player. And then we have a motive for the murder, and a pattern. Someone orchestrating the effort of people getting back at the ones they think did them wrong." Ellie felt like she was rambling.

Jordan, however, had gotten the point.

"That reeks of Darby and his punishments. But he's gone, and so is his fan club."

"Yet, Judy is once again at the center of all this. I'm sorry. This might not even be important, but I thought it was something to consider..."

"It definitely is. We'll keep this in mind."

Lieutenant Daniels passed them by, stopped and turned around. "Detective Carpenter. Could you please come to my office for a moment?"

"Yes, Ma'am," Jordan said.

Ellie was left wondering if she might face some criticism—but it wasn't like they had gone into a dangerous situation together. The department would have to hire even more in order to ensure she and Jordan never worked on cases together.

❧

"We were just exchanging the latest from our respective suspects...I can assure you, Ellie is up to the task."

Daniels held up a hand. "I'm not questioning that. As Lieutenant Carroll said, it's all hands on deck with this one, and we're glad Detective Harding is back at work. I wanted to check if you knew about this."

She moved her screen so Jordan could take a look at the headline with Jill Allen's name in the byline.

That was quick.

A City Remembers, the headline read, the focus being on Jensen Baker's family and friends dealing with the events. Jill had done her homework. Pratt indeed claimed that he'd seen the errors of his ways, but the ones who had been hurt by his actions weren't having it.

"With some things, there is no second chance," Jordan commented.

"True."

She realized that Daniels was still waiting for an answer, and she saw no harm in telling the truth.

"You understand that my connection with Pratt is not something I like to discuss, even less at work. He asked my biological mother if she would testify for him. She got scared and asked me for advice. We handled it."

"Yeah." It sounded like a half sigh. "This took a toll on everyone of us, but I know it was worse for those who worked the case, those who were close to Officer Baker, and especially you."

That made Jordan grit her teeth, an instinctive reaction.

"Sure. You and your unit didn't have an easy time either...Still, what you're saying is that this could backfire. I get it. We just couldn't sit around and do nothing."

"I wish you had come to me or Lieutenant Carroll first, that's all. No one with a basic understanding of Mr. Pratt's case would believe it's a good idea to release him."

"Then we're on the same page."

"Oh, we are. Next time, I'd prefer a heads-up, and I'd like you to pass that on to Detectives Harding, Henderson, and Doss."

This time, Jordan had a hard time keeping a poker face. Daniels had done her homework. Her instincts were right on the money as well.

"I'm sorry," she said.

"I expect this to blow over. Again, I understand. I just need you to keep me in the loop when it's more than a private matter."

"I'll keep it in mind."

"Thank you. And good work with Hastings."

"Thanks."

Chapter Seventeen

T hanks to that quick exchange of information with Jordan, Ellie had another angle to work with. First of all, though, she had Hastings detail the events at the amusement park.

"Man, they were wasted already," he said. "They saw us and started running. Then one of the guys took out his gun and...He just shot Randy. Another one had a chainsaw. I swear I didn't know."

Ellie had heard quite a few stories in her career, some bizarre, gruesome, some obvious lies—this would go right into the top five. For now, she wanted as many details as possible, but she couldn't help thinking what kind of person would be drawn to this game, even before it turned to murder and mutilation.

"And it never occurred to you that might be a bit harsh for...potentially getting someone fired?"

"I told you I didn't know! They found Todd and knocked him out. One of them drove away with him. I don't know what happened after that."

"You were there though when Randy was shot, and they cut off his hand."

He paled a little but nodded. "Yes."

"Neither you nor Jimmy tried to intervene, to help him?"

"It was like an out of body experience!" Dylan Hastings claimed. "I didn't expect this to happen…and they said that we were not to talk to anyone. Those are the rules. Anything can happen to you, any time."

"You obviously changed your mind. Why?"

Hastings shook his head. "I don't want to go to prison for the rest of my life for a prank, you know? I was mad at Randy, but I didn't want him to die."

"Did you help bury the body? You know where it is?"

He hesitated, prompting a stern look from the lawyer.

"I can show you."

Together with Detective Wu, Jordan learned the origins and rules of the clowns' game. The deeper they dove into it, the more it became obvious that this would be bigger than a local murder—but it would also give them a way in. Jimmy Bryan, who had been so courageous to scare a class of kindergarteners, was showing them how.

"I hung out with Dylan a few times," he explained. "He told me about a few sites that have these horror movies, and I checked some of them out. I didn't know about the game until I got the email with the invitation."

"To do what exactly?" Wu asked.

"Play a prank on someone. Scare them a little. You fill in a form and say what they did, and you get a number and an assignment from the game master. They assign random numbers to teams, give you the details, and you're good to go. Once you're done, it's over."

"How many times did you do this?" Jordan frowned.

"Just this once with Randy. And like I told you, I didn't know he was going to get killed! I had no idea either that they would put me together with Dylan. I thought staying anonymous was the point."

Jordan exchanged a look with her colleague. She had a hunch. If one player could identify another, they would turn on each other, and no one would be the wiser as to who the elusive master of the game was.

"Okay, Jimmy. You're going to show our techs the sites, and we'll figure out how to get to that form and open a new session," she decided. "Detective?" she addressed Wu.

He followed her into the observation area.

"All right," she continued, "while we are setting this up, I'll try to get a hold of the A.D.A., see what she can do about warrants for the address where the game origins from."

Wu nodded. "I can update the lieutenant."

For a moment, Jordan had all forgotten about their conversation regarding Pratt. She would have liked to forget about Pratt altogether, but apparently that wasn't in the stars

"You do that. I'll join you as soon as possible."

She found Valerie heading out, catching her in the doorway.

"Hey, Val, wait."

"I take it you are not about to extend a dinner invitation," she said with a sigh.

"Sorry, no. We have two suspects who have a lot to say about a morbid game they were invited to by email. So…"

"You always come to me with that pesky internet stuff. All right, you know what to do. Get the paperwork ready, and I'll see what I can do."

"Thank you. You're the best."

"That's what my girlfriend says, and she must be right."

"Yeah, that's…I'll go get that paperwork started."

Valerie left, laughing on her way out.

Jordan went back to her desk, then knocked on the lieutenant's office door. Wu was still with Daniels.

"Hey. I was just about to start the paperwork to get us those warrants," she said.

"Good." Daniels got up from behind her desk. "Meanwhile, Hastings told Detective Harding where to find Fowler's body. They're on their way. Henderson and Doss will focus on Fisher. He seems to be the missing link in all of this. Okay. Go to the tech lab, talk to Crawford, and tell her team everything you need. Tomorrow, you'll get yourself an invitation to that game."

After the gruesome find of the severed hand, the grounds of the amusement park had been turned upside down, to the chagrin of the company that was going to build on them. The location of Randy Fowler's body was five miles away in a wooded area dense with shrubs and dying trees. It wasn't a place where people walked their dogs, or children played, and so the grave had not been discovered until now.

Ellie wasn't particularly queasy, but given what she knew of the story, her stomach lurched when she saw the partly decomposed body, shreds of fabric sticking to it. There was nothing left for Fowler's grandmother to identify him.

A game.

Hastings and Bryan might be willing to talk now that they didn't see much of an alternative, but they, too, needed to be held accountable.

A freaking game.

She thought back to her conversation with Jordan, about the M.O. of their city's most infamous serial killer. Punishment. They might have been able to chalk it up to criminal minds thinking alike, but there was the matter of Carl Fisher, "Shawn" seeking out Judy Lawrence.

"Harding."

She jumped at the sound of Murphy's voice behind her. "We drive by Mrs. Fowler's on the way back?" he asked.

"Yes," she said. She wanted to go anywhere but there, to deliver the news. It was part of the job.

⁕

After setting things up with Anna Crawford and her team, they were close to calling it a day. Derek was finishing up some notes at his desk. Jordan could have been out of the building already. She was unsure what was holding her back.

"What's the matter?" Derek asked. "Something that cannot wait until tomorrow?"

Jordan halted her pacing, amazed at how well he had come to know her over the years. Even the latest shake-ups in their workplace didn't make a difference.

"Maybe it can. I'm not sure. Bryan is back in holding, right?"

"Yes, and you, and all of us need to eat sometime. We have to wait on Esposito, but everything else is set up for tomorrow."

"I know."

"So, what is it?"

"People like that don't slow down. It's the opposite. They escalate."

"Okay. Your point is..."

"That final challenge? The emails he showed us seem to support it, but think about it. Sneaking around a school, scaring some preschoolers. You go from kidnapping and murder to that? I don't buy it."

Derek sat up straighter.

141

"You think they were going to target one of the children—or the teacher?"

"I'm not sure. But I think Bryan lied to us. They want to get out of this as easily as possible, and if they both stick to the story, that might work for them to some extent. They didn't know what was going to happen, they were scared..."

"Nevertheless, they helped cover up a murder," he reminded her. "It's not going to be that easy."

"I just want to make sure we didn't miss anything. I want to talk to the teacher again and see if anything jumps out regarding those kids."

"You might be right. Or it's all about random violence and terrorizing people."

"Yeah."

"Not to change the subject but is there any news regarding Pratt?" he asked. "I saw the headline."

"You are changing the subject, but no. I suppose that it ends there."

"It should," he said. "People have suffered enough from this. Including you."

Jordan assumed that he was mostly talking about Kate, and Jensen's family. She knew no one blamed her for sharing genes with a criminal, but it was a relief to hear him say it.

"What do you want to do about Bryan?"

"I guess it's one more thing on the long list for tomorrow. Check the teacher and kids first, see what we can get from the game 'masters,'" she made quotation marks with her fingers, "and go from there."

"Dinner's at the *SEVEN*?"

"Yes. Our daughter is waiting for us."

At the *SEVEN*, Ellie was surprised to find Derek and Maria with Meri in the private room that they often used for dinners after work.

Jordan who had come in behind her, joked, "I'll have to have a word with my parents for giving my baby to just anyone."

"Hey, talk to the Godfather. I'm just here for a juicy burger," Maria returned.

Derek handed a wriggling Meri to Ellie who couldn't help thinking how things had changed since she became part of the group. Derek was still dating Maria when Ellie and Jordan got together. Now he was married to her best friend, and Maria in a relationship with A.D.A Valerie Esposito. They had made it through close calls, but on the other side, there was so much to be grateful for.

Kate came in a few minutes later, slumping into the chair Derek pulled for her. "Why isn't it Friday already?" Obviously not expecting an answer, she added, "Forget about it. How would I know the difference anyway?"

He whispered something to her that made her smile and took her coat.

"White wine?"

"Oh yes, please."

"You're ready to order?" Jack, who had just joined them, asked.

One of the things to be grateful for, Ellie reflected, was an evening with their friends and family, even in the midst of the chaos surrounding them. Pratt's scheming might add an additional layer of stress, but they knew they could count on each other.

After they got home and Meri's bedtime rituals were completed, the evening went in a direction more interesting than Ellie had expected.

"I'm really sorry you had to deal with Mrs. Fowler today," Jordan said as they were sitting at the kitchen table. "How did she take it?"

Ellie shrugged. "She's grieving. It's hard on her, but I think this gives her a bit of closure at least. She'll have more when we catch all of them."

"Yeah. We will."

"Tomorrow's going to be a long day. We should probably go to bed."

"We should," Jordan agreed.

They retreated to the bedroom not much later, but despite good intentions, Ellie didn't think that sleep was going to happen any time soon.

Perhaps they both needed a reminder that no matter how much cruelty and ignorance they were confronted with on the day job, there was a safe space they could always return to.

"So, you caught Jimmy Bryan lying, and you're going to prove it," she said, watching as Jordan opened a drawer for some sexy nightwear to put on over her panties. Ellie found the item quite distracting, though she kept her thoughts on track.

"That's the plan." Jordan said, closing the drawer. "Shouldn't be so hard now that we have the email, thanks to Anna. I can't believe he thought we couldn't recover it just because he deleted it. I knew there was something else. You want anything?" she asked since Ellie was still in a towel.

"No. I'm going to sleep naked," Ellie declared, not ready to end the shop talk. "But wow, you picked up on that...There's still a lot I can learn from you."

"Oh, I'm sure." Jordan didn't make too much of an effort to hide her amusement.

"Come on, I'm trying to have a professional conversation here."

"I know. The context just lends itself for that." Jordan pulled back the covers and lay down next to her. "I'm sorry. I know you had a bit of a crash course, because Waters got himself kicked out, and he wasn't much help before that. It's true what Carroll, Daniels and everyone else have told you. You have great instincts...You can still learn from me." That last part was a bit tongue in cheek. Ellie leaned closer, running her hand over the nightgown's silky fabric.

"I'll be paying attention, but I think I dropped the ball here. When did you buy this? I thought this wasn't your style, not that I'm complaining."

"Last week. I don't know, I guess I was happy it fit." Jordan sounded a tad rueful.

"It fits perfectly."

Ellie hadn't seen her struggle much with weight issues during and after her pregnancy, but a hospital stay and subsequent sick leave after her return to work had been challenging. Things were good now. They just needed to solve this case—and for Pratt to keep quiet.

Easy, wasn't it?

"You think you might want to take it off again?"

❧

"Mr. Bryan, this is A.D.A. Esposito," Jordan introduced Valerie.

"I take it you're ready to offer my client a deal," Bryan's lawyer surmised.

"We'll circle back to that in a minute. I'd just like to confirm a few things with you, Mr. Bryan. You said that the kindergarten was supposed to be your final challenge of the game. After that, you would no longer be obliged to play as long as you kept quiet. Is that correct?"

"That's all in my statement. Yes, it's correct."

"Good. The place was chosen randomly, your task to sneak around in a clown's mask, get their attention, have the police involved."

"I told you all of that already."

"I assume the A.D.A. is familiar with the statement," the lawyer added. "What's the hold-up, Detective?"

"It was all in the email you showed us, Mr. Bryan. This one?" She took a printout out of a folder and gave it to him. He read over it and nodded.

"Or was it this one the game masters sent you later? The one that's a bit clearer in its instructions?"

Bryan just stared at her slack jawed.

"What is this? Have you verified it?"

"It's not my first day on the job. We have verified that this was sent from the same account."

"I didn't know. I didn't read it. I did the challenge and then you arrested me."

"You received and read the email five hours before your arrest," Jordan told him what they already knew. "The kindergarten teacher is Claire Franklin, and she was one of the people targeted in the game. Bonus points for broken glass and blood. That was the challenge, to hurt Claire and or those children."

"No, no, you're getting this all wrong."

"Stop talking," his lawyer advised in a stern tone. "Detective Carpenter, I'd like to have a moment with my client."

"Of course. Mr. Bryan, we know that there is no final challenge. You're supposed to play indefinitely, but you can help us end this. You can help yourself and tell the truth."

She got up, and Valerie did the same.

Chapter Eighteen

C laire Franklin confirmed that her ex-boyfriend Barry Brooks had shown up at her workplace a few times, asking for a second chance. She'd been on the verge of involving the police but didn't when he stopped coming around.

"I thought he was over it. I had a security guard talk to him once, and I really thought he got the message."

She gave them his address though.

"We're finally making progress," Jordan pointed out when she and Wu were back in the car. "We drop by Barry's and invite him for a chat?"

"How about I drop you off at the station? You can pick up your car and go see him, meanwhile I take care of Morgan?" he suggested.

"Good idea."

The account from which the game invitations had been sent to Jimmy Bryan was registered to a Jeffrey Morgan. He had given a P.O. Box to open his account, but they had found an address for him too. And they could prove that Morgan, aka the game master, had plans more dire than "pranks" for the final challenge. More pressure on Bryan and Hastings—she hoped it would lead to something substantial. Preferably the person who had started the murder game.

Derek and Maria were still working hard on finding Fisher.

If they could find the missing "clowns" they'd be able to solve various cases.

That left the question of how many others were playing the game, in and beyond the city.

With Halloween fast approaching, a day where many families would be out on the street, they didn't have a lot of time left.

Jordan wondered if it wasn't a good idea to cancel trick-or-treating for this year.

⁂

By lunch break, she felt a bit less optimistic. Bryan had decided it was in his best interest to clam up, and Hastings had nothing to add to the story. Barry Brooks had agreed to come to the station, but he wasn't talking either and had asked for a lawyer.

Wu had called her to tell her that Jeffrey Morgan wasn't at his apartment, and he'd be setting up surveillance.

She stood in front of the board they'd created. Morgan. Carl "Shawn" Fisher. Brooks. Hastings, Bryan.

And the victims, Randy and Jenkins, Todd, Lisa, and those who were lucky enough to just be on the other side of a dumb "prank."

"You want to join us for lunch?" Maria asked behind her. Jordan turned to see her and Derek come in. Maria was carrying a box of Halloween candy.

"Wow, will that be lunch?" Jordan commented.

"Well, it's not the expensive kind, but you know you want some."

"I don't know. I think I'll find Ellie and go for a salad somewhere." She allowed herself a moment of remembering Ellie's appreciative gaze on her, a far more uplifting thought than when Shriver had sent her expensive chocolates. "You got anything on Fisher?" she asked before either of them could respond.

"Guy's fallen off the face off the earth," Derek said, sounding disgusted. "Is there any chance I could join you for that salad? I will not go near that." He gestured towards the box of bite-sized chocolate bars.

Maria shrugged. "Suit yourself. I'll go find someone who appreciates them, and me. See you later."

"Sure. How's it going on your side?" he addressed Jordan. "Since you're a lot less excited than earlier, I take it you hit a wall with Bryan?"

"Not just with him. There's something deeper to all of this," she said. "I'll get there, but first I need food."

<hr />

"What else is there?" Ellie asked after they'd given their orders. "I saw Valerie earlier. As for the Jenkins case, Hastings' DNA was on the mask, but that's not enough. And they've all decided to stop talking?"

"If only we could get to Jeffrey Morgan," Jordan said with a frown. "We'll be watching that P.O. box, but if he's local, he might have figured out that some of his players got arrested."

"Maybe not yet. If it's one guy, he can't be everywhere at the same time," Derek mused.

"Something still doesn't fit. When Bryan filled out that form, he chose Randy for his victim, Fisher wanted Jenkins out of the way, and Hastings is involved again? If Barry was a player, he didn't do the task himself. So, they were trying to improve the game, so everyone had an alibi?"

"That's quite Machiavellian," Ellie commented. "Like *Strangers on a Train*."

"Right," Derek said. "You do my crime, I do yours."

"Maybe that's what Morgan, the game master, had in mind. He might not have enough players signing up to pull it off, so they had to use the same people."

"It's possible," Jordan agreed. "If the number is limited, that would be a silver lining."

Their meals arrived, and they ate in silence for a while. Ellie changed gears, returning to a subject that had been on her mind for some time.

"I think we might have to look into daycare for Meri," she said. "It's been working so far, but Kate is swamped right now, and Jack and Pauline have lots of work with the bar already."

"Yeah, Kate is busy," Derek agreed. "Law school is a lot. She loves Meri, too, we all do, but I understand it's not enough in the long run. We're in awe of how you two manage."

"Making it up as we go a lot of the time," Jordan said. "I've never felt so clueless in my life, but we seem to be doing on okay job."

"Yes. One can only hope."

They changed the subject after that. Ellie made a mental note to call Kate later, maybe have her over for dinner sometime soon. Not to be nosy, but to make sure her friend was okay.

Jordan was about to leave, Ellie already waiting for her in the car, when her cell phone rang. Seeing the caller was Kathryn, she answered.

"Jordan, I'm so glad I could reach you." She sounded rattled, which was never a good thing. With Kathryn, it was worse, alarming her immediately.

"What happened?"

"TJ tried to call me again, I refused. Then his lawyer showed up on my doorstep when Jim wasn't home."

"What did he say? He didn't threaten you? He can't do that."

She made a sign to Ellie who got out on her side, walked around, and slid into the driver's seat. Jordan climbed into the passenger seat and fastened her seatbelt.

"No. I don't know," Kathryn answered, sounding unsure in the matter. "He tried to talk me into it, to listen to TJ, saying he regrets what he did."

"He was paid to say that," Jordan scoffed. The fact that the man had gone to the trouble of seeking Kathryn out, after Allen's article, disturbed her. "He can't make you do anything, you understand that, right?"

"Do I need a lawyer?"

"No, you don't."

On the other end, Kathryn took a deep breath. "Thank you. I hate bothering you with this, but...He kept going on and on about how TJ wanted to turn his life around and apologize to the people he's hurt. I didn't know what to believe anymore."

"I do. He tried to kill both of us, remember? And before that, he teamed up with a criminal who murdered a cop and shot several others. I was at that scene, Mom, and I'm telling you he's not going to get out."

Ellie kept her eyes on the road, but she seemed as startled as Jordan was at addressing Kathryn this way. So was Kathryn, and for several seconds, silence dragged on.

"Okay. I was hoping you'd say that." Ironic, above all, that Kathryn needed her to remind her of the truth. "I'll be more careful, I swear. That lawyer guy, he might want to talk to you too."

"Then I'll tell him the same thing. If he keeps coming around, let me know. We'll file a complaint."

"You'd do that?"

"Of course. I promise, that will be the end of it, and we can all move on with our lives."

"Thank you. I hope you have a good evening anyway."

"You too. I'll talk to you soon. Sorry about that," she said to Ellie after ending the call. "Too damn many ghosts."

"No kidding," Ellie agreed.

⁂

After Pauline had left, they waited for dinner to heat up, meanwhile watching an episode of *My Little Pony* with Meri. She might not understand the whole plot, but the cartoon made her happy, and Jordan was happy to keep things simple for the moment. That kind of peace proved to be elusive.

Thank God she and Ellie were married in the eyes of the law, and Kathryn had no interest in messing with their lives. Not that anyone would hand over a child to a criminal grandparent, just like that. Would they?

No one had thought he would even try after Jill Allen's article. On the other hand, TJ Pratt had no interest in a family, his biological one, or any. He'd made that clear when he held a gun to Kathryn's head the last time Jordan had seen him outside of a courtroom. He had gotten the sentence he deserved, appropriate for his crimes. In an imperfect system, that didn't always happen, but the system hadn't failed Kate, or the Bakers, or the other cops that got hurt in the ambush.

They had to make sure nothing changed. If the lawyer wanted to talk to her, she would make the time.

"You're far away," Ellie whispered, brushing her hand over Meri's hair.

"I'm fine. Kathryn is easily swayed. I'm not. I'll protect our family any way I have to."

If that was a tad melodramatic, Ellie didn't call her out on it. Perhaps she was worried enough not to.

The next morning, Ellie drove them to work. Their route led past a house where a scene from a famous horror movie was displayed, a plastic hand reaching out from a pretend grave. It made her shudder. There had been no more clown sightings. Likely they were aware of the arrests and were laying low. She hoped that she and her colleagues could keep the city safe for trick-or-treating...but there was the danger that the players might slip away.

They were someone's neighbor, co-worker. It was an unsettling thought, but then again, their attitude wasn't new—just their attire was.

Next to her, Jordan was silent, checking her phone.

Ellie was equally concerned about TJ Pratt's renewed efforts. She knew that for Jordan, there was a lot of shame attached to her family history. She didn't want to make her feel any worse than she already did, but there was a lawyer who thought Pratt might have a shot. If that was the case, what could happen?

At least, at the station everyone had settled in regarding their assignments and new colleagues, and Atwood didn't seem inclined to bring any more Halloween gag gifts to work after the clown case took on unexpected dimensions.

Both Carroll and Daniels were in this morning's briefing, listening to the update from the detectives.

Maria had brought what was left of the Halloween chocolates, and that morning, no one was joking about it.

"We're still watching Jeffrey Morgan's apartment and the P.O. Box," Wu said. "So far, nothing."

"And no trace of Carl Fisher?" Carroll asked.

Maria shook her head. "We widened the search. The media has been on it for a while. We will find him eventually."

"You're sure he's still around?"

She had an answer for Daniels. "If he's a player, literally, in this, yes, I think so—because of Ms. Lawrence. Then again, someone higher up in the game might have taken him out."

It wasn't something Ellie wanted to think about, that there might be more bodies buried across the city as part of the game. She had come to a point where she found it hard to maintain the anger at these men—she was tired of their attitude. They didn't care who they were hurting, feeling self-righteous in their actions. A few years down the line, and it could have been Meri in that kindergarten.

As if picking up on her thought, Jordan said, "We know that Claire Franklin was the main target, but I want to go over the list again, see if there's any other connection to the names on the board."

"You do that," Daniels said. "If that's all...Get back to work, and good luck."

They could all use it. Halloween had arrived.

Chapter Nineteen

W u had left for the break room with Murphy. Waiting at her desk, Jordan looked once again over the list of kindergarteners Claire Franklin had provided. Broken glass. Blood.

What was she missing? Besides the children's names, there was also a column with the parents' names, and how to reach them.

"Douglas Clarkson. Why does that name sound familiar?" Ellie had appeared behind her with a coffee. Jordan nearly jumped to her feet.

"That's it! You're the best. Clarkson. Of course." Emma Clarkson was one of the pre-schoolers, her dad Douglas "Doug" Clarkson, the owner of the company that was building the apartment complex and a parking lot where the amusement park used to be. She took a sip, nearly burning her tongue.

"Which brings us back to Todd and Randy, the people who were most bummed about the park being torn down. One of them is dead, the other was kidnapped by the clowns."

"I'm sorry, that's all I have," Ellie said.

"No, it's good. It's in here somewhere."

"You want to talk to him again?"

"It's an idea. I'm just waiting for Wu."

"Okay. Let me know what you find."

⚜

They started the drive in silence, until Wu surprised her.

"I think the supervisors, and most of us will be happy to never hear that name again, but if we're going to work together every day, it should be clear. We had no idea about Shriver."

"I never thought you did. Why are you bringing this up now?" she asked, genuinely curious.

"Apparently, he's been spreading rumors, about Major Crimes, and Daniels. She doesn't deserve that."

Jordan understood a bit more about where he was coming from.

"Don't sweat it. People like him hide in plain sight."

"Sure, but we of all people should be able to see through them, don't you think?"

"It's not always that easy." She wondered if that was a cop-out. Regarding Waters whose antics had turned into sexual assault. And Atwood, who had crossed the line more than once, but still came to work every day.

Noah Shriver. Wu didn't dispute her statement, but it was fairly obvious that they'd asked themselves some of the same questions. "We try to do better. That's all we can do."

He nodded. They had arrived at their location which put an end to the exchange. Jordan couldn't help wondering what Shriver was gaining from still pushing those rumors, and if he cared about the damage he'd done to the reputation of his unit.

Cliff Waters still thought he was the victim.

Mr. Clarkson emerged from his office while they were still talking to the secretary who had tried her best to stall them.

"That's okay, Elaine," he said. "I have a few minutes. The police you said...oh, it's you. Detective. I'm sorry, I forgot your name."

"It's Carpenter. Mr. Clarkson, this won't take long. We just have a few questions."

"If it's about the project, all is in motion now. We're good."

"I'm glad to hear that. You were informed about the incident at your daughter's pre-school?"

He looked haunted for a few seconds. "Those stupid clowns again? Yes, of course. Are you any closer to arresting them?"

"I'm sorry I can't talk about an ongoing investigation," she said. "Have you received any more threats? Anyone trying to extort or blackmail you?"

"That's oddly specific." He cast a look at his secretary who was now on the phone. "Let's go into my office."

They followed him into a spacious room where he gestured for them to sit down. "I was going to file a police report, but...then the incident at Emma's kindergarten happened, and we wanted to make sure she was okay." He took a photo from a folder that showed a placard for the apartment building. Scrawled across it in black paint were the words, *It Will Burn*.

"We've had stuff like this before, but with what happened at the park...I guess now that you're here, you could take care of it?"

⁂

"I can't believe he didn't contact us over this," Jordan said when they were on the way back to the station.

"He was worried about this daughter," Wu, who was driving, reminded her.

"I understand that, but...That's a direct threat. It could put his workers at risk."

"Yeah, and owners of corporations always think of their workers first," he deadpanned.

Jordan couldn't help but laugh. "You have a point there. All right. We'll add it to the never-ending list."

"Good catch on Clarkson though. We'll definitely have to do more digging on that connection."

Clarkson, another name to add to the board. It should have been there to begin with, Jordan thought. As if on cue, her cell phone rang.

"Hey," Derek said. "Ellie told us you were seeing the owner of the construction company? Anything from that?"

"A few more pieces of the puzzle, nothing earth-shattering yet. You didn't call just to ask about that, did you?"

"No. Fisher was spotted at a gas station on the corner of Twelfth and Maple. Squad cars are on the way, and we'll be there in a few minutes. We have roadblocks in place too. He's not going to get out of the city."

"That's what I like to hear. There's a chance we could wrap this up before trick-or-treating?"

"I thought you weren't going to take Meri."

"It's mostly going to be a stroll around the neighborhood, and it's pretty quiet there. We haven't exactly been the most social of neighbors, so this might be an opportunity. You and Kate want to come around later?"

"Maybe. I'll ask her," he said. "It all depends on how long this takes."

"Yeah...look, I know that gas station. We're not far away. How about we meet you there?"

To Detective Wu, she said, "Fisher has to have money, to pull off all those shenanigans. He is at the center of all this. What if he is Jeffrey Morgan?"

"Wait a second," Derek told her as they were walking along the back of the gas station where a camera had captured Carl Fisher. "Fowler played a prank on him that nearly cost him the car. He threatened to sue, then...he orchestrated the game using mostly Fowler's colleagues?"

"Is it really so far off? They went after Todd and Lisa too because of the whole triangle—I wouldn't call it love. What if Fisher is simply a jealous possessive asshole who can't stand to lose?"

"He gets Jenkins killed because the poor guy is taking too much of Judy's time, Randy Fowler because of the car, and Todd and Lisa...what's the difference here? And where is the connection to Clarkson?"

"The latter, I don't know yet. But perhaps they meant to kill Todd, and Lisa too."

"You have the sunniest outlook on things as always," he commented dryly. "Let's say that it's true—and it's Fisher behind all of this?"

"We've dealt with criminals who escaped arrest for a long time." Like TJ Pratt? "The clown masks, involving others, it just makes it more flashy."

"He goes around killing people, and they stand by."

Jordan shrugged. "I didn't say I have everything figured out, but having Fisher in custody would go a long way to put pressure on the others."

"Truer words..."

"Hey guys." Officer Casey Lyons came running towards them. "Guess what we found in the restroom."

They didn't have to guess hard, as she was holding the mask in a plastic bag.

Jordan cursed. "How many of those does he have?"

"One thing is for sure," Casey said. "None of my kids is getting one."

"Perhaps you'd like to bring them to a quiet residential neighborhood?" Jordan suggested. "If this is ever over."

❦

On the bright side, Hastings and Bryan hadn't made bail. Less of a bright side, Fisher had slipped off the radar again, despite everyone's best efforts. Casey and her husband were going to bring over their two younger kids. The older teenager had declared she was too old for trick-or-treating. Derek and Kate would spend the evening with them as well, and they could all do the envisioned stroll in the neighborhood.

They had exchanged a few niceties with their next-door neighbors before. Ellie wasn't sure if they knew their names, or professions…Well, perhaps the latter, because they'd been in the paper a time or two.

The plan was to go to a few houses, then come back home and heat up the lasagna Kathryn had cooked for them the other day when Ellie was on sick leave.

Kate and Derek had just come in when Casey's husband Jeff parked their car. The couple, and a young Supergirl and Harley Quinn emerged.

"How cute is that?" Kate commented from the window. "I used to love dressing up, but this year I don't have the energy. Maybe next year, what do you say, Meri?"

Meri seemed in agreement, and, fortunately comfortable in her soft, warm kitten costume.

"We could do a party," Ellie suggested. "I was going to get my wife a Wonder Woman costume, but she declined."

"That's too bad," Kate and Derek said nearly in unison. Jordan rolled her eyes and went to open the door to their other guests. They all came to the living area a moment later.

"Hey," Casey greeted them. "These two could barely contain their excitement. I think you can tell who they are?"

"Of course. Supergirl and Harley Quinn. You look great." The girls beamed at Jordan's praise. "Anna, Madison, this is Meri."

Ellie suppressed a smile. They sure were polite, and they hadn't seen her before, but she thought the prospect of candy was a lot more appealing to them than meeting someone else's baby.

"All right," she said. "We're complete. Who's ready to hunt for some candy?"

Ellie and Kate fell a bit behind as they walked along the decorated houses.

"You must be looking forward to the time after your exams," she said. "Maybe you two could get on the boat for a bit—or go to the cabin?" They had once taken a weekend at the cabins Derek's uncle owned, though a murder had cut that vacation short. "Someone needs to make better memories in that place."

"Sure, but it's not us anytime soon," Kate said wryly. "Do you have any idea how many bookings Jackson got since the murder up there? The perfect setting for a Christmas vacation, I guess. But no, we haven't thought of anything yet. We've both been busy, and we won't take the boat out until spring."

Ellie noticed that she looked pale. "Is everything okay?"

"Look who's asking. You've just recovered from a concussion. But yeah, I'm okay. Still pissed that Pratt even entertains the idea of getting himself out of prison."

"I can imagine," Ellie said carefully.

"Yeah. Derek has been great in all of this, trying to take my mind off it. It's been a lot. I'm really tired, and I'm only chasing legal precedents, not killer clowns."

"There is that. We're making progress, but it's slower than we would like. Bizarre stuff. At least, at the end of the day we get to go home to the little one."

"Meri is the best," Kate agreed, smiling as they watched the next-door neighbors fussing over her.

"She really is. And every moment goes by so fast." Perhaps she was really overreacting, and Kate would be fine once her exams were over and she could get a reasonable amount of sleep. Pratt's last-ditch effort had rattled all of them, a reminder to focus on what really counted.

Anna and Madison got their buckets filled. Meri looked happy, too, taking it all in with a wide-eyed expression. No urgent text or call—it looked like the city could have a peaceful Halloween celebration after all.

Jordan had seen the family in their driveway a time or two and said hello. The teenage daughter drove her bike past their house on most days in the morning. She didn't recognize the van parked in their driveway. Maybe they were having a dinner party.

Seeing that Meri was starting to get tired, she was ready to call it a night. They'd pretty much made the rounds in their small community, and she was surprised how many of the neighbors were aware of them. The couple two houses away had even extended a dinner invitation, something she found oddly touching.

Perhaps they had a tendency to huddle within their own bubble, and given the sometimes strange things they saw on the job, who could blame them?

She had to smile at the idea of her and Ellie having dinner with their neighbors in their other, suburban living, bubble. She'd never imagined it.

Jordan rang the doorbell. After a few heartbeats, a man in his forties answered. Now she wished she remembered the names of the couple.

"Trick-or-treat," Anna and Madison sing-songed.

He smiled. "We didn't have a lot of visitors tonight, so we have lots of candy left over. Could you wait here a second?"

He turned around and went back in, closing the door without locking, but not before Jordan caught a glimpse at the reflection in a hallway mirror. It jolted her into action.

"Get the kids out of here right away," she whispered to Ellie. "They're at least two, with guns, and they're holding them hostage."

Chapter Twenty

O f the adults, Casey's husband Jeff was the only one who had never worked in law enforcement, but he understood that there was no time to question or argue. He and Kate hurried to usher the children back to Jordan and Ellie's home, where they would use Kate's key to get inside, and wait for further instructions.

Everyone had stepped away from the door. Derek was on the phone, requesting back-up.

Daniels' warnings flashed in Jordan's mind, and she had to admit the woman was right.

"Ellie, I need you to go home with them. We'll wait here until back-up arrives."

"What? Jeff and Kate will be fine."

Jordan took her aside, her grip a bit tighter than necessary. She let go when Ellie winced. "I won't be. Please, trust me on this."

Ellie gave her a long, quizzical look.

"I need you to go home and be with Meri, handle things from there."

To her relief, Ellie simply nodded and turned to sprint into the direction where they'd come from. Halloween wouldn't be so quiet in their neighborhood after all, after their neighbors had the bad luck of being chosen for the game. Either way, it would be the final one for the players. *Enough.*

The tactical team arrived within minutes, and Jordan and Derek met them at a small intersection down the block where the hostage takers wouldn't have eyes on them. They got Mrs. Dennison's number from her provider.

"I can call her phone and see what the situation looks like inside. I got a glimpse of two intruders. There might be more."

While she was talking to the captain of the squad team, the neighborhood was being secured.

"Okay," he said. "Go ahead but be careful."

Jordan called the number, aware of the tension, everyone's eyes on her. After six rings, the phone was answered. All she could hear was rustling and white noise for a few seconds, then Mrs. Dennison answered.

"Hello?" She had the voice of someone trying hard to mask the fact she'd been crying. It also sounded like the intruders had put her on speakerphone. Jordan knew she had to think fast.

"Hey, it's Jordan Carpenter, your neighbor. I know this is strange, but…In the last group of kids that came to your door tonight, how many were there? We were wondering if we could turn off the lights."

At first, she feared her tactic wouldn't work, but then Mrs. Dennison answered,

"Oh, less than four kids. Those were the last ones in a while. So yes, you probably could turn it off."

"Great, thank you. We'll just watch a bit of TV in the living room. You too, maybe?"

"Yes, but I still have to cook dinner."

Despite the tense situation, she barely suppressed a smile. The woman was thinking quick too.

"We'll check the front to see if more children show up," Mrs. Dennison added.

"You do that. And let's get together soon, okay?"

"I'd love that," the woman said before the call was interrupted.

Jordan turned to the captain, and Lieutenant Daniels, who had arrived while she was on the phone.

"There's three of them. She said yes to the living room, and cooking dinner means there's someone in the kitchen too," she translated. "They're watching the front of the house. If we can create a diversion…"

"Still tricky," Daniels said. "What if they move them?"

"They have them in the living room. I caught a glimpse earlier, but I don't think they realize we're here yet. I could go to the front door—"

"And do what? Are you out of your mind?" That tone, especially in front of a supervisor, was unusual for Derek. She could feel her jaw drop.

"You have a better idea, let's hear it. But don't wait too long, because I'll bet you that this part of the game involves killing my neighbors. There's a fifteen-year-old girl in there."

"Your point being? You have a girl at home that's barely a year old."

"Detectives," Daniels said sharply. "Not the time." In the resulting tense silence she added, "Are you absolutely sure that this is related?"

"The email Jimmy Bryan lied about. In the original version, they envisioned something like this. Yes, I'm sure it's related."

Daniels hesitated for a split-second, before she turned to the leader of the SWAT team. "I'm for a diversion out front, but it can't be Detective Carpenter. They'll know something is up. What do you think?"

He nodded.

"All right," she said.

Jordan followed Derek to the back of the house where men and women in SWAT gear were already in position, waiting for the signal. She was going to talk to him later. No matter how many close calls had happened lately, now was not the time to get over-protective. Each of them had to do their jobs.

"Why did we have to go?" Madison asked once more after Meri was ready for bed. Ellie had come downstairs to check on Casey's family while Kate stayed with Meri. "When is Mom coming back?"

"Soon," her father tried to assure her.

"I'm hungry," Anna chimed in.

Ellie exchanged a look with Casey's husband, certain that he felt the same. Her stomach was in knots, food the last thing on her mind. However, the longer they could make the girls believe that nothing much was wrong, the better.

"We wanted to order in when everyone's back, but would you like some applesauce? Or chips?" The girl's face brightened. "Can I have some candy too?"

Jeff Lyons sighed. "You're going to spoil your appetite, but I guess we can make an exception for one day. Just don't eat everything all at once."

"I'll prepare something. I'll be right back," Ellie promised. In the kitchen, she leaned her head against the fridge, startled when she sensed someone behind her.

"Sorry," Jeff said. "I just wanted to see if I can help you with something."

"Yes, thank you. You think they might like a glass of milk—or juice?"

"That would be great, thanks."

Ellie put glasses and a plate on the table, and took out a bag of chips, some cheese, and cherry tomatoes.

"Anything new?" he asked. Ellie had called the station to be updated. Officer Martin who was on the front desk tonight, couldn't tell her much. They'd send a SWAT team. No news yet.

"It's torture," he said. "I know that the job could involve stuff like this, on any day...but sometimes I think it's better not to think about it."

Ellie didn't blame him, though she didn't point out that she felt like she should have stayed. But that was Daniels' point, right? It couldn't work that way. Carroll didn't want to have them out in the field together either, though there had been moments when they had no choice. Or did they? Jordan had been adamant about sending her home.

"They'll be fine," she said. "They know what to do."

"Yeah."

He took a carton of milk out of the fridge and poured two glasses. "Let's hope they're not going to be sick."

"Would you like anything?"

He shook his head and left to head back to the children.

Torture, Ellie thought, and then her phone rang.

❦

The moment had arrived.

"Trick or treat," Casey, who had rung the doorbell, gave the sign. At the back of the house, one of the members of the team carefully slid open the glass door connecting a spacious deck to a dining area. One by one, they filed in, Jordan and Derek last.

The two of them hadn't made it to the living room when they heard a gun go off, glass shattering, and shouted commands.

Seconds later, they both joined the team in the living room, seeing two men facedown on the carpet. Both of them, including a sulking Carl Fisher, were being cuffed. Him, Jordan had expected. She had to admit that she hadn't counted on seeing Todd Williams, who was being dragged in from the kitchen by one of their colleagues.

"He was trying to get away."

"Emphasis on trying, huh? It's over, Todd," she told him. "You lost."

He didn't react other than giving her a sullen stare.

Her instincts had told her that something was off about him but not fully prepared her for how far he'd been willing to go. They'd deal with him later.

Jordan headed towards the family's teenage daughter, while Derek talked to Mrs. Dennison. Paramedics tended to her unconscious husband. All three had been tied up and gagged with duct tape, a bloody head wound a sign that Mr. Dennison had tried to take on the hostage takers. Jordan thought of that day in the woods, finding Ellie, and she had to suppress a shudder. Pushing the memory aside, she focused on the girl in front of her. She seemed physically unharmed, just in shock.

"I'm going to remove this, okay," Jordan told her, referring to the duct tape over her mouth. "I'll be careful." It was going to hurt anyway, she knew from experience. Best to do it quick. "You remember me? Ellie and I live down the street. I often see you on your bike." In one swift move, the tape came off, eliciting a yelp from the teenager. "You did great. That was the hardest part. You all did great," Jordan added, taking a quick look around. She was glad to see that Mr. Dennison had come to, helped onto a gurney by the paramedics. Derek spoke softly to Mrs. Dennison as he cut the duct tape off her wrists and ankles.

Jordan started to do the same for the teenage daughter.

"Zoe, right?" They had gathered that information earlier, but Jordan felt a tad embarrassed that she hadn't known before. Zoe nodded, her eyes incredibly wide. "Okay, Zoe, those paramedics will check you out, and they'll take all of you to the hospital."

"Dad?" she whispered. "They hit him."

"The doctors will take good care of him, and all of you. We'll talk some more soon, okay?"

"Okay. Thank you."

When she was free, she all but jumped to her feet and ran over to her mother who had gotten to her feet as well, and the two embraced.

"Great job," Jordan told Mrs. Dennison. "You were a big help in ending this as soon as it did."

The other woman gave her a teary, but grateful smile. "I kinda wish you meant that when you said we'd get together. I'd be happy to make you and your family dinner."

"Not for this, it's our job—but it would be nice to have dinner sometime soon. I'm afraid Ellie and I haven't been very social."

"I imagine you're busy." Mrs. Dennison didn't elaborate. Jordan could imagine that she had seen some of the headlines that came with recent cases.

Their neighbor cast a look at the paramedics waiting. "I assume you need our statements?"

"Hospital first, and then it will be just the bare bones for tonight. We'll take care of the rest tomorrow."

Todd Williams, in on it from the beginning with Carl Fisher.

"We know these men. They're not going to get away."

"Why our home? You think it was random."

"We don't know yet," Jordan said, unwilling to share her theory with her neighbor. In her mind, it was no coincidence that they had chosen the quiet neighborhood that Ellie and Jordan called home, for the final game.

They'd get those answers eventually.

Chapter
Twenty-One

J ordan came home to find everything in the best possible
order. Meri was sleeping in her bed, Casey's girls sat quietly
in a corner playing a game with their tablets, the table was set,
and take-out delivery called.

Regardless of the fact that Jeff and Kate, too, had a lot of
questions, she asked Ellie to come upstairs with her. In the
bedroom, she pulled her into a quick, tight embrace.

"I'm sorry. But it was the right thing to do."

"I know," Ellie admitted with a sigh. "I understand what
Daniels is trying to do, and even though we were off duty, the
principle is the same. I get it. One of us needed to be with Meri,
and, well, you have seniority."

"I do." Jordan gave her a relieved smile. "Thank you for taking care of everything. You won't be missing anything tomorrow—Daniels will want everyone on this."

"Then we better get something to eat. They should be here
in ten minutes or so."

"Good. Everything quiet here?"

"Yes. The girls never noticed." Ellie shook her head as if unsure what else to say next about this bizarre turn of events.

In hindsight not completely unexpected, Jordan thought, but still bizarre.

"That's a good thing. We were lucky to shut this down without anyone else getting killed. Mr. Dennison will be all right."

"Thank God. And you know what's a very bright side? We won't be seeing any clowns for a long time to come," Ellie said, and they both laughed.

"Right. Let's hope tomorrow will the last day we'll have to deal with those."

"Todd Williams, really? So he faked his abduction, and the story about the love triangle was all a hoax?"

"It would seem so. We'll know more tomorrow. And here's dinner," Jordan said when the doorbell rang. "Speaking of which, we got an invitation earlier."

❦

Jordan had left before elaborating on her cryptic statement. Deciding it was probably not that important, Ellie made a beeline for Meri's room and then went downstairs as well.

After distributing pizza and beer to their friends, Ellie sat down next to Casey, who shook her head in disbelief. "You know, you were one of the best trainees I ever had, but we're never going to do any social activities with you anymore. You guys can't do peaceful and quiet."

Ellie took a sip of her beer as she observed Jordan and Derek standing by the window.

"I'm too tired to know if that's a joke, but if it's not, I can't blame you. Meri's first trick-or-treating, not that we'll let her have a lot of candy yet."

"I'm sorry if that sounded bad. I'm glad we're all here...I just spoke with my oldest, and she's blissfully oblivious of it all."

"They called it a game. Incredible, right?"

"They'll soon realize what losers they are," Casey said. "You all did a great job on this."

Ellie hoped she was right. She was grateful that the Dennison family had come out of it alive, but others had not been so fortunate.

Randy Fowler.

Ronald Jenkins.

Lisa had been taken in for questioning and let go. Judy Lawrence would have to learn about Carl Fisher's true motive.

She cast another look over at Jordan, still in deep conversation with her partner.

Tonight likely had brought up some issues for them, and she dared guess that they had little to do with clowns.

⁂

"That was a bit harsh earlier," Jordan said, referring to their interaction at the Dennisons' front door, "but you didn't have to pay for the pizza."

Derek made a dismissive gesture. "We hang out here, and at your parents' bar all the time, and it's been on the house more than once. Don't worry about it."

"All right. Thanks."

"You're welcome. And I'm sorry."

"Thank you."

"You were really going to knock on that door?"

"Come on. I made a suggestion. I wasn't insisting. Time was running out."

"It always is, isn't it?"

"What's that supposed to mean?" Jordan asked, more confused than offended.

"Nothing." Derek's answer was too quick.

Jordan wasn't entirely convinced that this would be the end of it. Come tomorrow, they'd both need their head in the game. She wasn't willing to let this, whatever this was, linger.

"Okay, what is really going on? This is not still about Joy Anne and— "

"That was pretty horrific, but no. It's just been a few long weeks since that first clown showed up."

"No kidding. It's over now."

Derek sighed. "The clowns, yes. Pratt, we can't be sure."

She was starting to have a better idea of where he was coming from.

"I'll be the first to admit, I have no use for this, but he'll realize eventually that his plan won't work."

"All the damage he did...That's not entirely gone."

"No. It's been rough on you and Kate. I understand." Jordan could read between the lines. Her partner and Ellie's best friend had gotten together under difficult circumstances, but their relationship was solid now. Pratt's scheming had rattled all of them. They had to remind themselves of the truth. "Whatever happened though, it was not your fault. It was Pratt's. And he'll stay locked up."

"Let's drink to that," Derek said, sounding grateful. He raised his bottle to clink it against hers.

She hoped she wasn't promising too much.

⁂

"Okay, let's do this." Jordan appeared almost cheery when she opened the door to the interrogation room.

Staying behind in the observation area, Ellie watched her walk inside with an air of confidence that never failed to impress her. She had reason to, but still.

"Hi, Mr. Bryan," Jordan said as she sat across from him.

Ellie could see her own, spell-bound reflection in the glass. He had no idea.

"I don't know why you wanted me here," he said. "Yes, I agreed to talk to you, but if you're just going to ask the same questions, I have nothing else to add."

"Sure. Just checking."

"That's all?" He laughed. "What a waste of taxpayer money."

"Well, we could argue about that. Scaring people for petty reasons, lying to the police...You could call that wasting taxpayer money. Or, I don't know, someone faking their own abduction?"

There was a minute change in his expression.

"Nobody faked anything," he said. "I told you over and over again I didn't want anything to do with that. Just pranks."

"Yeah, I get you. The only question is now, who's going to go down for those pranks, because I can assure you, someone will. Maybe Dylan? Maybe you? But it will also be interesting to talk to Carl and Todd about this after we found them holding a family hostage, threatening to kill them."

He remained stubborn, but Ellie could see his fingers twitch.

"Okay," Jordan said in the same calm tone. "That's up to you. I guess we're going to wrap up with Todd now. It's probably going to be more interesting."

She got to her feet but didn't even make it all across the room.

"I'll talk to you! I'm not going down for all his crap."

"The thing is, we've heard this before."

"I'm serious! He doesn't give a damn about Lisa, or anyone. It's all just random. He likes scaring people. I swear I had no idea he wanted to kill them too."

"He went pretty far for a game."

"Well, you believed him, didn't you? He got a kick out of that. He set Randy up. He and Carl set us all up."

"They might not have the last laugh after all if you and Dylan come clean." Jordan sat again and leaned back in her chair. "I've got time."

"She's got this," Maria commented. "I guess it's up to us listening to Todd rambling why he felt justified terrorizing the city."

"I'll be right there," Ellie said, only to have her colleague respond quickly.

"It's fine. Derek and I will do this. Wu got Fisher. I guess you could finish up with Dylan Hastings, see if he has anything to add? I think if you go with the Carpenter playbook, you'll be just fine."

She left, and Ellie stood for a few seconds, unsure about the entirety of the information she'd received.

She didn't doubt though that Jordan's strategy would work on Hastings. Everything else was beyond the scope of their job.

Chapter
Twenty-Two

I n the late afternoon, Carroll and Daniels asked everyone
into the briefing room. There was an air of relief and triumph in the group. Once again, their work had confirmed what
they'd experienced over and over again. Some of these men were
eager to boast about what they'd gotten away with.

"Finally...lots of random violence," Jordan concluded.
"Fisher planted the mask at Jenkins' house after killing him. He
claims he didn't know about Judy Lawrence's story until they'd
already started dating, but he was mad at Jenkins for taking so
much of her time."

Ellie listened, coming to her own, sobering conclusions. This
time, there was no elaborate punishment scheme. They called
it a game...but everyone had done their jobs and put an end to
the murderous antics. They still had to deal with the other issue
that kept coming up. This went beyond the job. It was about
protecting their family, and she would do whatever it took.

As the detectives shared their conclusions one by one, Ellie
formulated a plan. She wasn't going to keep it a secret from
Jordan, though she assumed she'd have some convincing to do.

Perhaps later, over a beer at the *SEVEN*, would be a good moment to approach the subject.

"No, absolutely not. This has nothing to do with you."

Under different circumstances, in a different time, Ellie might have found this insulting, but she knew the impact the recent developments had on Jordan.

"I'll pretend you didn't say that, because you know, it has everything to do with me, with us. Please, hear me out. I'm not saying I look forward to it, but I think I should be the one doing it."

"Why?" Jordan took another sip of her beer. "I'm sorry, you're right. We both have to deal with this somehow, but..."

"TJ Pratt is a criminal, and he's serving this sentence for a reason. You need to get the idea out of your head that there's anyone in the world who blames you for his mess. Not any of our colleagues, our friends, certainly not me. Hell, not even Atwood," she said when the officer walked past them without a greeting.

She could tell by the fact that Jordan wasn't trying to argue she was on to something. Ellie wished she wasn't right about this, after the years they'd spent together. The truth was Pratt hadn't been a subject often. Jordan had enough on her plate figuring out how to deal with Kathryn's desire to make amends. They'd come a long way, but Pratt's agenda might put a strain on their new-found relationship.

"I see your point. I swear. But I don't want—"

"I've done more dangerous things. No, wait, that didn't come out right. It's not going to be dangerous in any way. And he won't see it coming."

"I don't know what to say."

"Help me out. Tell me everything I need to know so we can put this to rest." Ellie laughed. "You don't like it, but I'm right on everything."

"When your spouse tells you that, it's usually time to stop arguing," Lieutenant Daniels who had joined them, joked. "Could I steal Detective Carpenter for a moment?"

"You definitely could," Jordan said. "As you can see, I'm losing the argument."

"I'll just find Kate," Ellie announced. "You're both right."

Jordan watched her walk away, amused, before she turned to her supervisor. "Can I buy you a drink? As an official welcome?"

Daniels shook her head with a smile. "Oh no, I can't do that. But I wanted to congratulate you on how you handled the closing of this case. This was close to home."

"True. At least no one got severely hurt—and it didn't happen *in* our home but thank you."

"You're welcome. And I want you to know I meant what I said the other day. There's a clear path up the ladder for you in this department."

"I'm glad to hear that." For the most part, Jordan had been comfortable, grateful she had managed to come back from the various challenges of the past year. Daniels' words made her wonder if she had become too comfortable. If she had the option, she'd certainly prefer to stay with the department rather than go with the job her ex had tried to sell her.

"Good." She eyed the glass Ellie had left on the counter, and for a moment, Jordan wondered if she was changing her mind about the drink. "You have a good evening, and please know that you can always come to me. I understand no one likes the reason for those recent changes, but that doesn't mean we can't make the best of them."

It was no mystery what, who, she was referring to.

"Shriver fooled all of us."

"Yes. Thank God that story is over."

Jordan picked up her glass and raised it.

"I'll see you Monday morning," Lieutenant Daniels said, taking a look around. "Your parents really did a great job with the rebuild."

"Thank you. Good night, Lieutenant."

With Pratt, Shriver, and the clowns behind bars, Daniels was right that it was time to focus on themselves, and their goals. Look who had the last laugh in the end?

She flagged the bartender for another drink and then went to find Ellie.

※

Ellie wasn't worried about meeting TJ Pratt. The only emotion she could identify was anger, because after everything he'd done, he was still looking for a way to avoid accountability. Place the blame on someone else. He hadn't pulled the trigger that day, but he had evaded arrest for some time. He would have killed Kathryn, if Jordan hadn't intervened.

He studied her curiously, and for a few seconds, she observed him in return. She remembered seeing him on a gurney. At that point, the danger was past. She and Kate had been assigned to guard a witness.

"Mr. Pratt, thank you for meeting me. We haven't met. I'm Jordan's wife."

"I'm not surprised." He smiled. "It looks like we both turned our lives around."

The idea that he and Jordan could have anything in common was stunning.

"About that. We know that you and your lawyer have contacted Mrs. Lawson for a possible testimony."

"Oh yes," Pratt said, sounding excited.

This was a guy who had been living in a trailer while sitting on a lot of money. She didn't trust him. He'd say anything to get out of prison.

"I understand Kathryn is a bit hesitant, but I think she'll come around. After all, Jordan is our daughter...and now that we have a grandchild...Did you bring pictures?"

"No."

"That's too bad. Next time maybe?"

Ellie leaned forward. "There's something I'd like you to pass on to your lawyer. Look, Jordan, and I, and Ms. McCarthy will all be happy to testify if you ever get a parole hearing. To be honest, I don't think it's likely, but just in case...We'll tell the board everything they need to know, and you will never get out."

"She forgave Kathryn, but she can't forgive me?"

"Kathryn isn't responsible for the death of a cop."

"But that was Ryder! He was convicted."

"And you helped him. That's not something any of us can forget, so please don't contact any of us again. Goodbye, Mr. Pratt."

A few minutes later, after leaving the block and getting her purse from the locker, she sat back in the car, next to Jordan.

"It's really over," she said. "He got the message." Jordan pulled her close. Ellie hoped that she, too, knew the truth. Saying it out loud never harmed. "I love you."

Jordan held on tighter for a few seconds before she pulled back. "I love you too, but let's get out of here, okay? I feel weird doing this in the parking lot of a prison."

"Sure. Let's get Meri and have a quiet evening."

"Sounds great to me."

A little over twenty-four hours after the visit from Detective Harding, TJ Pratt was still livid. He had come up with the plan over a year ago. He had studied for it.

He didn't reach out to Kathryn, the mother of his daughter, until he was certain he had a story to offer to her. Kathryn had always been a sucker for a good story, and he'd almost had her. For the most part, her relationship with Jordan Carpenter, the girl from the trailer turned cop, hadn't been great. What had changed? Why would they be joining forces in sabotaging him and the new life he deserved, all of a sudden? Occupied with his thoughts, he almost ran into someone, the response predictably aggressive.

"Hey! Watch where you're going! What's the matter with you?"

He hated it when they were younger and fitter than him. He shouldn't be in here, having to watch his back 24/7.

"None of your business," Pratt muttered, and found himself with his back against the wall the next moment. "What the fuck—"

It occurred to him that there was no one else in the hallway...but cameras, right? He stared into the man's wild eyes, aware that he had to come up with another plan quick, or this wasn't going to end well for him.

"I have money," he said.

To his surprise, the other man let him go, laughing as if he'd made a good joke.

"I don't care about money."

The glint of the blade came out of nowhere.

Sirens, lockdown, frantic footsteps. He lay on his cot, hands linked behind his head, smiling.

So, you want to defend her, but how far would you really go to protect her? Kill somebody?

I win.

Ellie didn't miss Lieutenant Carroll's party at the *SEVEN*. She had been worried about the timing of his retirement, wondering what it meant for him, and everyone in her unit. Seeing her boss laughing at something his wife said, relaxed in a way she didn't think she'd ever seen him, she realized that no one had made this choice for him.

Lieutenant Daniels was more than motivated to do the best possible job, and she had already shown her dedication to keep them working as efficiently as they could. A win for everyone.

Jordan ended her phone call and joined her at the table.

"How's everything at home? What did Ariel say?" Ellie asked, and Jordan's guilty expression told her immediately that she'd guessed right. "Don't feel bad about it. I would have checked in a couple of minutes."

"She said that she's probably taken care of more babies than I have. A bit cheeky, but I have to admit she's not wrong. Everything's fine."

"Good. We won't stay that long. The lieutenant will understand."

"I sure do." He had come over to their table. "And thank you for catching those guys before the party. I knew I could count on you."

"I hope that includes all of us," Maria commented, and he laughed.

"Of course. You did me proud."

The change in atmosphere had registered with everyone. Ellie could tell that Jordan was just as touched, if not more, because she and Derek had worked with Carroll for quite a few more years.

In the midst of the solemn moment, Lieutenant Daniels arrived, her phone in hand.

"Detective Doss, could I have a moment?" She and Maria went over to another corner where Detectives Wu and Murphy were waiting already. The four of them conferred, looking serious.

A few minutes later, they got ready to leave, and Maria, already in her coat, came over to them.

"I wish you all the best, Lieutenant. I'm sorry, but I have to go."

"What happened?" Ellie asked.

Maria hesitated, which only increased her concern. Seeing that Jordan was paying attention to something Derek said, she took Ellie aside and whispered, "Daniels got a call from the prison. TJ Pratt was murdered. I really need to go."

For a few seconds, Ellie was speechless. She hadn't expected anything like that. She'd have to find her words soon, though, because she'd be the one to deliver the news to Jordan.

For the moment, she was grateful that they, and their closest friends, all had alibis.

About the Author

B arbara Winkes writes sapphic crime drama and Christmas romance. She loves writing characters who get the job done, whether it's stopping a predator or saving cherished traditions—while still making time for love. She lives with her wife in Quebec City.

barbarawinkes.com

Also by Barbara Winkes

Luce Allen Mysteries
In Harm's Way
Under Pressure

The Crossing Lines Trilogy
Undercover
Redemption
Vengeance

The Connected Series
Promised to the Queen
Drawn to the Enemy
Tempted by the Protector
Saved by the Heiress

Carpenter/Harding
Indiscretions
Insinuations
Incisions
Intrusions

BARBARA WINKES

Initiations
Intentions
Infatuations
Impressions
Implications
Infractions
Incidents
Illusions

Kelli & Merin Romantic Suspense
Thunder
Rain

Lord and Burton
Clean Slate

Standalone
The Amnesia Project